DAMNATION FOR BEGINNERS

A Novella of the Deepgate Codex

DAMNATION FOR BEGINNERS

A Novella of the Deepgate Codex

ALAN CAMPBELL

SUBTERRANEAN PRESS ✦✦ 2012

First Edition

ISBN
978-1-59606-439-3

Subterranean Press
PO Box 190106
Burton, MI 48519

www.subterraneanpress.com

NOW

THE BOOK HAD WARNED him to expect manifestations—especially objects growing out of his body while he slept—but that didn't prevent him from panicking the first time it happened. He had woken from a feverish dream in which he and Carol had taken a picnic in the meadow near Alderney, only to discover that daises had sprouted from his knees.

A wave of revulsion overcame him. The flowers themselves didn't bother him as much as the queer tactile sensations he knew would be associated with them. Jack touched one of the flowers, and shivered. Those tiny green caules and petals brimmed with his own living nerves. It had, he supposed, been like brushing a tumour. These daisies were now as much a part of his body as his own skin.

What did the book say about getting rid of them?

The moment he thought about the book, he found that he was clutching it in his hand. The gilt letters stamped upon the cover gleamed brightly: *Damnation for Beginners by Charles Rain*. Out of habit, Jack plucked his handkerchief from his breast pocket and used it to flip open the cover before he remembered that he didn't need to do that any more. The small cotton square no longer offered him any protection. He tucked it away again, and set the book down on his lap.

Marley's inscription adorned the first page; it was becoming neater every time he glanced at it. Almost all of the fly-spattered ink had vanished from the margins, leaving rows of near perfect letters stamped across a crisp, white paper rectangle.

If I can't talk you out of this, Jack, maybe this book can. If not, at least you'll know what you're getting yourself into. Damnation is not something to be undertaken lightly—for any reason.

Regards,
Marley.

Jack used his bare fingers to rifle through the pages, hunting for the appropriate section. But the words inside flowed and changed as he tried to read them. He stopped and took a deep breath. He had studied this volume. He *knew it* word for word. All he had to do was remember. *Page 82, Section Nine, Deformations of the...*

The text resolved itself into a structure he recognised.

Section Nine
Deformations of the Conscious Soul

Deformations of the Conscious Soul most often happen during lapses of concentration, such as when dreaming, but they can also be achieved by a deliberate act of will. Attempts to physically remove unnatural obtrusions will cause bleeding and pain, and should be avoided. The Conscious Soul will return to its natural state in time, although the following breathing exercises can often facilitate—

Jack knew the passage by heart, just as he knew every other passage in the book, but seeing it there in black and white reassured him. He didn't bother with the breathing exercises. He thought: *I can do this. It is a system that can be learned, mastered, and manipulated, like any other system. Damnation has a formula.*

He set the book down, and yet he could still feel its leather-clad board pressing against the wooden top of the night table. He had yet to become used to this faintly disturbing sensation; it reminded him of a story about a crippled miner whose missing arm still ached. In Jack's case, both the book and the night table were part of his body, too, as was everything else in the room.

White boarding surrounded him, geometric patchworks composed of hundreds of square and rectangular panels. He knew without counting that there would be 6561 of them, because this was his favourite number. Tall white curtains along one wall concealed windows, but these were pressed directly up against the brick wall of his neighbour's dwelling, and so offered him no view. The room possessed numerous other useless exits. 81 of the panels boasted keyholes and small brass handles, however opening these revealed nothing but further rectangles of brickwork. These particular portals appeared to have moved since the last time he'd paid them any attention. He had a strong impression that they were searching for a gap in the surrounding walls. *Steered by the subconscious.* That was to be expected, he supposed. Around the edges of the chamber stood further subconsciously significant objects: a replica of Carol's fancy dresser, the lilac-painted wood now polished to a ceramic sheen; an ink bottle and a pen; a rocking chair; and an empty copper coal scuttle. Jack pondered the significance of these things. The dresser was easy: Carol had brought it with her when they'd moved to Highcliffe, and he'd always loathed the way the dust gathered in the carvings. This represented his guilt, then. The ink bottle must be a regurgitation from the part of his mind concerned with work. The chair—his grandmother had owned a chair like that, and it had always unnerved him. And the empty coal scuttle? That one bothered him more than the others. It looked clean and bright on the surface, but he knew there would be horrors lurking inside. A small portrait of Carol rested against the skirting board. Her painted face had been smiling originally, but Jack's imagination had now creased her brow with disapproval. She was frowning at the torture implements scattered across the floor.

The knives, pliers, clubs and hatchets had been here when he's first woken up in Hell. Symptoms of his rage, no doubt. He couldn't use *these* particular objects on his intended victim: they were part of his corporeal subconscious, after all. But they mimicked the tools he'd thought about gathering together in real life—the steel all polished to surgical perfection, the blades as thin as gas. In the middle of this murderous display loomed its gruesome centrepiece: an iron maiden as tall as a man. It waited with its hinged doors open wide and its belly aglitter with spikes. The floorboards beneath it had started to bruise under its tremendous weight.

"I'm not responsible for that," he said to his wife's portrait. "I don't even know where it came from."

Her disapproval deepened.

Jack got up from the bed and walked over to the spiked cabinet. He ran his hand across the pitted iron surface. Then he knelt and pressed a hand against the purpled floorboards surrounding the base. A fierce jolt of pain startled him. The location of this sensation, like most others down here, was hard to pinpoint. It had come, simultaneously, from both his arm and the floor. The room itself was a ghost limb.

He tried to steady his breathing again. Was he actually breathing? He didn't know. But holding his breath for any length of time still made him redden, and panic, and finally gasp. All he had to do was take the necessary time to understand his environment. *Breathe in. Breathe out. One, two, one two.* He would figure out this system, and then he would use it to his advantage.

Beyond the walls, floor, and ceiling, Jack could sense the other rooms surrounding him, compressing his own small space in Hell. It felt like he was lying under a pile of bodies—which, he supposed, was close enough to the truth.

Section Two
You are your Surroundings

Your subconscious manifests itself as your surroundings. This is a natural defence mechanism to protect the conscious element of your soul—the artefact you will come to regard as your body—from the millions of other damned spirits around you. You must learn to control your state of mind. In Hell, imagined stimuli become very real and very dangerous. Wish for a fire in your hearth, and its flames will crisp the corners of your soul. Fear a stranger's knock upon your door, and you will immediately hear such a report, for he will be standing outside, and his intentions will be whatever you—in your worst nightmares—have imagined them to be.

Jack glanced at the iron maiden and wondered what would happen if he stepped inside and slammed its vicious doors closed behind him. Could a mind be punctured by spikes that were a manifestation of that same mind? What happened when someone trapped in Hell tried to kill themselves? He tried to push the thoughts from his head. Lately, he'd been thinking far too much about suicide.

THREE WEEKS AGO

FRANKLY, IT WAS OUTRAGEOUS! How horrible these people were to make her wait in this heat! Mistress Angelina shuffled forward another step, using the compliant form they'd given her to fan her face. Given her? They'd practically *shoved* it at her. The queue looked barely shorter than it had done ten minutes ago. It stretched from the Document Office three hundred yards behind her and ran all the way up to the very edge of the cliff.

Hundreds of people waited in line, all sweating, their clothes powdered white with the dust from the nearby mines. She could hear the rumble of Henry Sill's great wheel coming from the head of the queue, and she could feel the shudder of the ore crushers deep in the earth below her feet, but she still couldn't see the infernal machine from here. The man in front was too tall for his own good. You couldn't help but notice the wheel from Cog City, of course—its enormous spokes flush against the rock face, endlessly turning like some ghastly fairground ride as it powered the corporation's whole gold mining operation. But there was little to see from up here on the Pandemerian plateau itself.

"How much longer do you think they'll be?" she asked the man in front of her.

"Not much longer," he said. "It's built up speed now."

Mistress Angelina tutted. "Really, it's a disgrace."

"At least it's not raining."

A spot of rain might actually have been a relief. It was only mid-morning, but the sun was already unbearable. You certainly felt it more up here, away from the sea breezes in Cog and Port Ellen. The air was thick with dust from the mines and more dust from the horses' hooves as the drivers halted their horrid little brickleback carriages to unload yet more people outside the Document Office; it nipped one's eyes and one's nostrils and hung over everything in an ochre pall. If she'd known it was going to be like this, she would never have worn her best frock.

The queue moved forward again.

"We're moving now," the man said. "The wheel's going at a fair clip."

"I can see that, thank you."

"Of course, that gives you less time to lodge your complaint."

"I shall take all the time I need," she replied.

He shrugged.

The people ahead of her began to move at a brisker pace. Mistress Angelina hurried to keep up, fearful of losing her hard-earned place amongst them, her sensible little boots struggling on this rocky ground. A moment later, she heard the voice of the wheel steward.

"Six to a cabin, quickly now."

And suddenly a space opened up before her. The steward herded people towards the edge of the precipice, where a wide boarding ramp extended across six feet of hazy air towards a small wooden cabin suspended from the top of the great wheel's rim. Identical cabins hung from the steelwork on either side, each stamped with Henry Sill's coat of arms above their open doorways. She recognised the stylised coin and garotte at once, of course. The same design was emblazoned across the top of her complaint form. But there on the cabin wall it seemed so much more vulgar. Did the man have to mark everything he owned? Beyond the wheel lay nothing but sky.

"Six to a cabin, quickly now."

Mistress Angelina watched as half a dozen people in front of her hurried across the embarkation ramp and ducked inside the cabin doorway. The wooden chambers never stopped moving, revolving slowly away as the vast wheel turned. It would carry its occupants all the way down down to the base of the cliff.

"Six to a cabin, quickly now."

Mistress Angelina felt a hand on her arm. Before she could protest, she found herself being propelled forwards along with a group of five others. Planks moaned under their boots as they crossed the ramp. She endured a moment of vertigo, whereupon she glimpsed the whole of Cog City spread out below her, the vast tremulous blue of the ocean beyond, and then she stepped into the gloom of the cabin.

Wickers of brass-work separated the bank staff from the public, with shallow wells sunk into the counter top to facilitate the exchange of paperwork. There were no lamps, only a bare hook in the ceiling to accommodate one. A window in the far wall provided some illumination, but it was scarcely enough to see by. And there was nowhere whatsoever to sit. Mistress Angelina walked straight up to an unoccupied teller, and pushed her complaint form towards him. He was a neat young man with close-cropped auburn hair and kind eyes—the sort of man who looked like he smiled a lot. But Mistress Angelina resolved not to let his appearance disarm her. He wore an immaculate grey suit with a small brass badge pinned to his lapel. The letters embossed there would presumably spell his name.

"My complaint," she said.

He glanced at the form. For a moment he seemed vaguely uncomfortable. Then he plucked a white handkerchief from his breast pocket, and used it to slide the printed sheet through the well towards him. "Miss Angelina Carin," he said, now smiling amiably. "I am obliged to inform you that we have about 90 seconds before the cabin reaches ground level, whereupon all customers must disembark. The Henry Sill Banking Corporation cannot be held liable for any injuries sustained by a customer who fails to disembark promptly."

"What?"

"We have a very limited time to deal with each customer complaint."

"What happens if I run out of time?"

"You'll just have to come back."

Mistress Angelina glared at him. "And queue up again?"

"I'm afraid so."

"But that's…"

"Please," the young teller said. "Let's see what I can do for you in the time we do have." He set his handkerchief aside, and his gaze shuttled rapidly across the complaint form. "It says here you borrowed 20 ducats…"

"Well…"

"…And you were supposed to repay the loan over three years, at two ducats per month. A total of 72 ducats."

"It was to buy a gown and cap for my grandson's graduation," Mistress Angelina said. "We could have hired one, but…well, you know how it is. Stephen deserved something a bit special for once. He's worked so hard for it, and I wanted to contribute."

The young man's expression softened, and he smiled again. His finger hovered over the form. "You have been repaying this loan now for…"

"Seven years and two months," Mistress Angelina said. "I've been trying to tell you people this for years, but nobody returns my letters. I've had nothing but threats and demands."

"You're not from Cog?"

"Amstire. It's a three day voyage by ship."

A clock on the wall behind the young man chimed, but he kept his full attention on the paperwork. "Your problem, Miss Carin," he said, "is one of overpayment."

"That's what I've been trying to tell you."

"You were supposed to make 36 payments… Unfortunately, you made 37."

Mistress Angelina exhaled pointedly. "I think you'll find I've made 86 payments."

"No, I mean, you sent us an extra payment after the three year term was up. That's the root of the problem." He sighed and glanced at the teller seated to his right, an older man with a caldera of grey hair. Then he looked back at her again. "Because that extra payment was over and in excess of your loan, the bank was forced to conclude that you intended us to hold that money for you. When this happens, the loan department automatically opens an account in your name."

Mistress Angelina nodded.

"The standard fee for opening an account without prior agreement is 40 ducats, which was deducted from the original two you sent us, leaving a debt of 38 ducats. Since this amounted to an unauthorized overdraft, it incurred a further administration fee of 25 ducats, and an additional maintenance fee of 10 ducats per month. Once you add on the primary, secondary and tertiary interest—deducting, of course, the two ducats you have been paying each month—the sum outstanding is 1882 ducats and three pennies. That's what you need to pay."

The clock on the wall chimed again.

"Do you have any assets you could sell to settle the debt?"

Mistress Angelina felt her legs weaken. "But I paid my loan," she said.

"You really need to speak to someone in Reclamation," the young man replied. "They'll sort out a payment plan, look at your assets if need be. Are you a home owner, Miss Carin?" He spread his hands. "Perhaps someone in your family…"

"You don't understand," she said. "I paid my loan."

The clock chimed once more.

"We're approaching the ground," the young man said. He wrote something across the top of the complaint form in careful, neat letters. "I've given you a new reference number, here. Hand this in to Reclamation after you disembark. They'll help you from here." He used his handkerchief to slide the form back through the slot.

Mistress Angelina just stared at it.

The clock began to chime repeatedly.

"Miss Carin? You need follow the other customers outside. Please disembark immediately."

Mistress Angelina continued to stare at the sheet of paper with its indecipherable scrawl of black ink across the top. The tick boxes. The little printed letters. All the words the woman in the Document Office had filled in for her. She didn't understand any of it. A metal band now seemed to be tightening around her chest, restricting her breathing. The clock was ringing frantically now. She had already forgotten what it meant.

"Please," the bank teller insisted. "Miss Carin. You have to leave *now*. There's a security—"

She heard a *snap*. A rush of air. Light flooded the room. And suddenly she was falling. She slammed against hard ground and heard another snap. She tasted dust; it stung her eyes and nose. Bright blue skies reeled overhead, and lines of steel and shadow. A spike of pain shot through her hip and she cried out. She spied the cabin six feet above her. Its floor had parted along its middle, leaving two sections swinging underneath on hinges. A trapdoor? It had opened underneath her, dropping her into the dusty space below the wheel and the disembarkation platform.

"Ma'am?"

Mistress Angelina crawled in the dirt.

"Do you need some help, Ma'am?"

She turned to see a fellow in overalls approaching across the hard-baked ground. "My hip," she wailed.

He crouched down beside her, and picked up her complaint form from the ground nearby. "Let's get you over to Reclamation, shall we?"

A DAY IN THE WHEEL

MARLEY HELD OUT HIS hand. "Five."

"She might be hurt."

"She'll be fine. You owe me five."

"But what if she broke something?"

"Hand's still empty, Jack."

Jack reached into his wallet, slipped out a clean five ducat note, and placed on the counter next to the other man's open palm. Through the open floor hatch he could see one of the disembarkation staff helping the old woman up. He began to relax a little.

"What's that now?" Marley said. "Three out of three?"

Jack made a dismissive gesture. "I don't want to do this any more."

"You love it really."

"No, I do not. We shouldn't be making money out of other people's misfortune."

Marley pocketed his winnings and laughed. "Everyone else is."

"That's no excuse." Jack dabbed his handkerchief against his brow. It seemed suddenly so much hotter in here. "How do you *always* know who's going to drop?"

Marley clasped his hands behind his head, and leaned back against the wall. "Seven years of experience," he said. "Firstly, that woman was clearly not from around here. You can tell by the clothes. And, secondly, old women never can make up their minds. Happens every time."

The cabin rocked slightly as it continued to climb. They had about 90 seconds of free time before they reached the top of the wheel and another group of customers alighted. Jack should have been utilising this moment to fill out his report, but he scrunched up his handkerchief and used it to give the counter top a quick polish instead. None of the other Complaint Officers showed any interest in the old lady's sudden departure. They'd seen it all before. But Jack's heart was only now starting to slow down. "I tried to warn her," he said.

"You did everything by the book," Marley replied. "But it was never going to make a difference with her. Some people just don't understand the system." Sunlight reflected off the top of the old timer's naked head, giving it the appearance of a great pink egg. "The longer you stay in this job, the more you realise that most people are idiots. What was her problem? Tertiary interest?"

"Overpayment."

Marley chuckled. "Beautiful."

Jack leaned forward on his stool and gave the grille a quick polish, too. A film of dust had gathered there. Through the open trapdoor in the floor, he could see the stream of people wandering away from the disembarkation platform at the base of the wheel. They were heading down the path towards the carriage rank and the administration buildings. The city of Cog spread out across the land below. Stone houses crusted the shoreline around the mouth of the Sill river, named after the pirate who had first discovered it. A short distance inland the waterway moated an island festooned with the red patchwork roofs of grand hotels and grander government offices, and the tall white spires of the cathedral. Four bridges stapled this island to the marble spine of Highcliffe in the north, and to Port Sellen in the south, where the harbour breakwaters cradled a flotilla of navy vessels.

Jack inhaled. The fresh scent of the sea came in through the trapdoor, dispelling the papery must of his surroundings. He had long been of the opinion that sea air was the cleanest air, and he took this moment to clear his lungs, listening to the ever-present squeak of the wheel's huge axle and the grumble of the ore crushers deep inside the cliff face. The other Complaint Officers were now busy with their reports, so he picked up his own pen and went back to work.

Morning became afternoon. The flow of customers never ceased. Jack dealt with them in ninety second intervals, deconstructing their complaints from behind his brass grille, patiently explaining to them the ins and outs of the Henry Sill Banking Corporation system, before sending them on their way again. Confusion over Tertiary Interest formed the bulk of his cases, which was to be expected. The Adjustment Bureau had been busy changing all of its customer mandates to incorporate this new account feature, whereupon an additional level of interest now applied to Secondary Interest, which had in turn been applied to Primary Interest. By funnelling all standard repayments outside these channels, the Bank ensured it could maintain the bulk of customer debt indefinitely, thus providing an endless stream of profit for its lone shareholder. Quaternary Interest, Jack suspected, would become standard by the end of the year in order to further increase margins.

He'd never had to deal with such blatant fiscal trickery during his time with Sanderson and Bree, but then Sanderson and Bree had crumbled when the recession hit and Mr Bree had caved in Mr Sanderson's skull with a ship-lantern-style paperweight. *Accountants*. One never could believe they were capable of extreme violence, until it actually happened.

It was almost four by the clock when Marley tapped five fingers on the counter to indicate his desire to make another wager. Jack scowled at the spot where the old man's fingers had touched the wood.

"Sorry," Marley whispered. "I forgot."

Jack quickly removed the blemish with his handkerchief. But by then the customer was standing behind the grille and it was already too late to rebuke Marley for trying to induce another wager. This new arrival wore the soiled overalls of a dockworker, or other heavy industry employee. To Jack's horror, the man's filthy hands were actually resting on the counter top.

Nevertheless, he managed to swallow his revulsion, and utter the disclaimer by rote. "…whereupon all customers must disembark. The Henry Sill Banking Corporation cannot be held liable for any injuries sustained by a customer who fails to disembark promptly."

"Your name is Aviso?" the man said, indicating Jack's name badge.

"That's correct, sir. May I see your complaint form?"

"Any relation to Carol Aviso?"

"She's my wife."

The customer smiled, and slid his paperwork under the grille. "Well, that's a damn relief, I don't mind telling you, sir. Your wife dealt with my mother's complaint. She was very helpful."

Jack raised his eyebrows. "Helpful?"

The man's smile broadened. "*Very helpful.*" He said this with the pointed emphasis of a fellow conspirator, implying that both he and Jack knew what he was referring to, but that it wasn't necessarily for public consumption.

Jack glanced over at Marley, but the old timer was busy dealing with his own customer. He examined the man's complaint form. "Mr...Everett. It says here that you borrowed 140 ducats six months ago"—he carried on reading—"and that there has been a problem with the repayments from...well, almost immediately. The bank received—"

"Is she not working today?"

"I'm sorry?"

"Your wife."

Jack pointed his pen at the wall behind the customer's head. "Six cabins behind this one."

"You don't work together?"

"We don't get to choose our cabins, Mr Everett." Jack returned his attention to the paperwork. "Now, according to this, the bank received the first payment back in—"

"I didn't borrow anything," Everett said. "My brother took out the loan. He died three weeks later."

Jack nodded. "I'm so sorry. However, you did agree to act as guarantor."

"No, I didn't."

"The mandate clearly—"

"I didn't know anything about the loan," Everett said. "I haven't spoken to my brother in years. I didn't even know he'd moved back to Pandemeria."

"Unfortunately, your name was added."

The customer's smile had long gone by now. "So what?" he said. "Why should I repay money I didn't borrow, money I didn't even know *he'd* borrowed until a week ago? How do I know my name is even *on* the agreement? They won't show it to me."

"It's bank policy," Jack said. "We can't give out the details of your brother's account."

The clock on the wall behind him chimed.

"*My brother's account,*" Everett said. "That's my point. I don't owe you people anything. I've never taken a loan in my life. If you want this money back, you can bloody well dig him up and ask him what the Hell he did with it."

Jack sighed. The loan documents had probably been adjusted post-mortem to add the brother as guarantor. How else could the bank be expected to recoup its losses? This meant that the paperwork would be in order, and if the paperwork was in order, then the mandate couldn't be challenged in court. This was actually a blessing for the customer. Since Henry Sill owned the courts, and therefore the verdicts, Mr Everett would save himself a fortune in legal fees.

"I'll give you a reference number to take to Reclamation," Jack said. "They'll be able to assist you from here. If your brother had any assets, then the sale of those will undoubtedly make a difference to the outstanding amount." Frankly, he doubted there *would* be assets, otherwise the bank wouldn't need to pursue the man standing before him. "Do you have any other family who could help? Your mother, perhaps?"

Mr Everett's face reddened. He bared his teeth. "*I didn't borrow any money.*"

"The bank needs to recoup its losses, Mr Everett."

The clock chimed again.

Mr Everett leaned close to the grille and spoke in a low, threatening tone: "I am not paying you one greasy ducat."

Jack recoiled from the torrent of breath, covering his mouth with his handkerchief. The other customers were already moving towards the door, ready to disembark. He glanced over to see Marley looking at him with a wry grin on his face. "I'm afraid we've run out of time," Jack said to Everett. "You'll have to take this up with Reclamation."

Everett snatched the paper from the counter. He glared at Jack a moment longer, then turned and joined the queue behind the door, just as the clock rung the disembarkation warning. A moment later, the door opened and the customers filed out.

Marley clasped his hands behind his head. "You should have taken my bet," he said. "You'd have won that one."

Carol finished her shift a few minutes after Jack. He waited for her at the disembarkation platform at the base of the wheel while the other employees wandered off towards the carriage rank and the administration buildings. When she caught up with him, she smiled and wrapped her arms around his neck. "What a day," she muttered.

He endured the hug for as long as he could bear, then disentangled himself. "I've had rather a bad day myself."

"What's wrong?"

He shook his head. "I'm just tired. Let's go."

They took a carriage down the hill through the Heights, past the miners' cottages and the fallen water tower. Jack wasn't in a mood to talk, but he sat patiently on his handkerchief and listened to Carol moan about her day: the bloody customers; her shift boss, Lineman, and how he shirked his own reports and left them all for her; Margaret Fischer and her attitude and that weird hair loss, which was probably a result of the cheap dyes she bought from the river market; and people shouldn't buy those dyes because the makers used river silt instead of muskrat. The horses' hooves clopped and the carriage wheels scraped, slid and rattled along the uneven ground.

Evening sunlight was sloping into the city by the time they reached Cog Island bridge.

"Is everything all right?" she asked.

Jack stared at the road. "Someone breathed on me," he said.

She laughed.

"He said he knew you, that you helped his mother with a complaint."

"Okay."

"It was the way he said it, though. You *helped* her, like you resolved it or something."

She didn't respond.

Jack turned to face her. For a moment she seemed pensive, but then she shook it off. "I don't remember anyone like that," she said. "What did he look like?"

"A dockworker," Jack said. "I don't think you actually met *him*. He was talking about something you did for his mother." He hesitated. "You didn't actually *resolve* a complaint, did you?"

"Of course not."

"Then why did he think you did?"

Carol shook her head. "I don't know anything about this, Jack. We get old women, and sometimes they're confused, and some of them even smile and thank us afterwards. But I send them all on to Reclamation just like I'm supposed to."

Jack gazed out at the passing façades.

"Do you think I'd jeopardise our careers?" she said.

"I'm sorry." Jack hesitated a moment, and then gave her an awkward hug. He could feel the sandpaper texture of her jacket under his fingers, but he tried not to flinch. He'd been getting better at that sort of thing recently. Carol, however, was unyielding in his arms, and remained that way throughout the rest of the journey, as if mere insinuations could calcify a woman's joints.

Cobbled lanes stitched Highcliffe and the Theatre District to a ridge north of the river. The horses strained to drag even such a delicate carriage up the steep inclines. The clatter of their iron-shod hooves ricocheted between the marble defiles like musket balls. At one point the driver dismounted from his sprung seat to guide the beasts around a cadre of Priests heading for the Temple of Rys, bowing his head as the cloaked forms flowed past. Carol ignored them entirely, gazing sullenly at a passing doorstep. With the sun now vanished behind the rooftops, the streets became noticeably cooler.

"We could go and see a play," Jack suggested.

"You?" she said. "Go and see a play?"

"It might cheer you up."

"I'm fine, Jack."

But clearly she wasn't. When they reached their apartment block, she left the carriage without a word, leaving Jack to pay the driver and pocket a handkerchief full of change.

"Methinks someone saw the notice board."

"*Methinks*?" Jack said.

Marley chuckled. "Why else are you so miserable? You heard about the sleepwheel."

They were taking their first 90 second break of the day. The sun had only just risen above the sea, and the chill of the night yet remained inside their cabin. Marley still had his scarf wrapped around his chin and was warming his ink pot in his hands. He looked, for all the world, like a common bandit.

"What sleepwheel?"

The old timer leaned back on his stool. "The Henry Sill Banking Corporation has just been granted town council permission for a second wheel. Like this one, but full of bunks. You climb up, and—"

"You're serious?"

"The notice is on the board."

"They were supposed to be building another bunkhouse."

"It *is* a bunkhouse." Marley gave him a rueful smile. "It just happens to crush ore at the same time. Or pump water from the mines, or...something useful, anyway. The notice doesn't actually say."

"They're going to have men working while they sleep?"

"That's the beauty of it," Marley said. "They'll use the bunk-house *between* shifts, so Mr Sill doesn't have to reduce their debts to the corporation. And it solves the problem of gold thefts, since *all* the miners now have to remain on site at all times."

"How can you sleep in 90 second intervals?"

"Ah, but the new wheel is going to be much bigger. And there's some sort of difference in gear ratios. I don't know the specifics."

Jack muttered under his breath,"What a world."

"I'm sorry?"

"Nothing," Jack said. "I suppose it's ingenious, in a way."

Marley nodded eagerly. "And that's only the beginning," he said in hushed tones of excitement. "There is talk of opening a branch of the bank in Hell."

Jack adopted a cynical expression.

"Some of the top people at Cog University think it's possi-ble," Marley went on. "Charles Rain reckons that if you spilled enough blood to make a portal, you would be able to send a living representative through. Henry Sill got right behind the project. It's a whole new territory for him."

"Who is Charles Rain?"

"The man who wrote the handbook on Hell. You've never heard of him?"

Jack hadn't.

"I'll lend you the book sometime," Marley said.

"But why open a branch there, anyway?" Jack said. "The damned don't have money, do they?"

"The new branch wouldn't deal with money," Marley said. "They'd trade in souls."

Jack just stared at him.

"Hell itself is entirely constructed from souls," Marley said. "The Mesmerists use them to construct their cities. And if something is useful, then it's a commodity."

Jack couldn't imagine King Menoa, the Lord of Hell, ever agreeing to such a proposal. Why should his Mesmerists trade for a commodity they could simply mine for themselves? If Hell was, as Marley had just pointed out, composed entirely from souls, then what would be the point of trading in them? He put this to Marley.

"Some souls have more value than others," Marley replied. "That said, I don't suppose Henry Sill would ever be allowed to expand into Menoa's territory without offering him something in return. The details all have to be worked out, I'm sure, but I wouldn't underestimate Mr Sill's persistence and passion in this thing. He has more money than all of the gods combined."

They worked for the next few hours without incident. Jack's customers brought him the usual complaints, while he sat behind his brass grille and gave them the standard answers. He tuned out the ever-present grumble of the ore crushers and lost himself in the paperwork. Of course, the fiscal labyrinth that kept the Henry Sill Banking Corporation in profit could not be navigated by its customers. That was its purpose. It was intended to confound. Monies borrowed; repayment schedules; demands and responses; aggregate and compound interest; charges and fines: Jack dealt with them all in a diligent fashion. He enjoyed working within a system with clear rules and boundaries, even if those boundaries changed biweekly to increase profit margins. Sanderson and Bree's system had been positively childlike by comparison. Patiently, he explained to customers why their accounts had been restructured in order to shuffle outstanding payments and fines into the three tier high interest channels. He explained why mandates had been adjusted, or no longer applied.

He explained why payments delayed by the bank itself incurred the same fines as those delayed by the customer and why the cost of an unauthorised sixty ducat overdraft had now increased to thirteen hundred ducats, with a twenty ducat charge for administration and a further ninety ducats for the necessary document re-management process, during which time the bank had a legal right to glean an additional nine ducats in primary interest and three more in secondary and tertiary interest and why authorised overdrafts would still be categorised as unauthorised if the Document Office failed to pass the relevant paperwork on to the Adjustment Bureau in time, which was, sadly, a regular occurrence and yet entirely preventable if only the customer had taken out Account Management Insurance.

Hadn't they enquired about Mr Sill's insurance products when they arranged the loan? Failure to do so could put their homes at risk.

Most of the customers Jack's department dealt with had reached the end of their use to the corporation. When all that could be wrung from a person had indeed been wrung, Jack gave them a reference number and filed their names and addresses to be passed on to Reclamation. The majority of people left the cabin quickly, wrapped in shrouds of gloom—but, on that particular morning, three of them remained long enough to trigger the security trapdoor. Marley gave up trying to get Jack to wager, but he still chuckled every time the floor opened and another unfortunate soul hit the dust. More often than not, he was the one who pulled the reset lever to close the trapdoor. The bank, he said, was planning to introduce a customer fee for this.

It was after the third customer had fallen, when Marley peered down through the open trapdoor and said, "That looks like Carol."

Jack rose from his stool to see for himself.

He spotted her standing beside the disembarkation platform. From her posture and animated hand gestures he knew she was being defensive about something. She appeared to be arguing with two men. One was lean, about Jack's age, while his companion looked older and stouter. Both of them wore dark suits and pudding bowl hats. Carol had spread her hands, as if to fend them off. She talked quickly, with a kind of desperate energy that was unusual for her. Jack couldn't hear what she was saying, but it was evident that she didn't want to be there.

"You didn't borrow money from the bank did you, Jack?"

"Of course not."

The old timer's expression remained grim. "They look like Reclamation Men to me."

"We didn't borrow..."

"What about Carol?"

Jack shook his head. "She's not a fool, Marley."

"Then it must be a misunderstanding." Marley didn't quite manage to say that with conviction.

Their own cabin rose higher above the platform with every passing moment. A further two minutes would elapse before it completed its revolution. Jack could do nothing but watch as the older of the two men took Carol by the arm and led her away. He lost sight of the trio momentarily among the great clutter of spokes, but soon spied them again walking towards the administration buildings. She didn't appear to be resisting, and yet her head hung low and her heeled shoes slipped and stumbled on the rocky ground.

COMPANY POLICY

JACK LEFT CABIN WHEN it reached the disembarkation platform, and manoeuvred his way though the crowd of customers filing down the stairs. He couldn't see Carol anywhere.

"Jack?"

He turned back to find their shift boss, Miles, frowning at him from the open doorway. "Where do you think you're going?"

"I'll be back soon," Jack said.

"I have to report it."

"Can't you just put me down for an extra shift? I'll make up the time."

The other man shook his head. "Still have to report it," he said. "Company policy."

Jack waved his hand dismissively. He took off across the hard packed ground in the direction of the administration buildings, passing under the shadow of the wooden tower that housed the great wheel's chains and gear assemblies. A slowly revolving steel shaft ran from the base of this structure into a tunnel in the rock face. The processor building itself, where rock from the mines was crushed and separated into waste and ore for leaching, lay underground. Eleven other tunnels punctured the cliff face at various heights, all connected by a wobbling lattice of ropes and walkways and ladders. He could hear the chime of hammers and picks coming from within, as Sill's miners clawed away at their debts with picks, wedges and hammers. A wailing siren warned of impending detonations somewhere deep within the earth.

The shock wave from those explosions shuddered through the ground just as Jack reached the entrance to the main administration building. A nondescript grey block, it housed the offices of Payroll, Taxes, Work Records, Recruitment, and Reclamation. He walked right past the queue of customers waiting outside, took out his handkerchief, and used it to turn the door handle.

The large woman behind the front desk did not look up from her typewriter. She was in her mid fifties and sported a remarkable sphere of orange-brown hair every bit as brash and fuzzy as something one might win at a travelling carnival. A huge red and pink floral dress constrained an unlikely collection of bulges. The stump of a burned-out cigarette wobbled between her lips as she struck the typewriter keys repeatedly with a single plump finger. Two doors leading into the interior of the building flanked her desk. In addition to the prerequisite coat of arms, each of these portals had been fitted with a large steel combination lock next to its handle. The woman's present client—a dowdy, middle-aged man wearing farmer's breeches and a cloth cap—sat on a tiny stool before her desk. He looked up as Jack approached, revealing a boil in his nostril the size and colour of a crab apple.

"I need to find my wife," Jack said to the woman.

She continued to hit her typewriter keys.

"Her name is Carol Aviso. There's been some sort of mix up with Reclamation."

The desk clerk slid the typewriter carriage back. "I'm presently dealing with a client," she said.

"I just need to know where she's been taken."

She ignored him for a while longer, then said, "We don't give out personal information. If your query concerns your wife, you'll need to ask her to come in here herself."

Jack closed his mouth, opened it, then closed it again. "You want me to ask her to come in, so that we can find out where she's been taken?"

The woman moved her lips, brandishing the cigarette stub like a tiny sabre. "Company policy."

Her client turned to Jack. "Do you mind?" he said. "I was here first."

Jack ignored him. "Is there someone else I can speak to?"

"Do you have an appointment?"

"No."

"Would you like to make an appointment?"

"Can't I just speak to someone now?"

"Not without an appointment."

Jack took a deep breath. "Alright. Please make me an appointment."

The desk clerk stopped typing. She reached into a small cardboard shelving unit on her desk and withdrew a sheet of paper. "Name?"

"Jack Aviso."

"Which administrative department manager do you wish to see?"

"I don't know."

Her weary gaze rolled up to his face. "I can't make you an appointment for you if you don't tell me who you want to see."

"Let me speak to someone in Reclamation."

She shook her head. "You'll need a reference number for that. You can obtain one from the Complaints Department."

Jack leaned closer to the desk and whispered. "I work in the Complaints Department."

"Then you should be aware of the policy."

This route wasn't going to get him anywhere. Reference numbers could only be issued to complainants who had an account with the bank. And of course neither Jack nor Carol had such an account. He might work for Henry Sill, but it made no sense to trust the man with his own hard-earned money. He thought for a moment.

"What if I had information regarding a particular customer's undisclosed assets?" he said. "You would be compelled to let me speak to Reclamation as a matter of urgency. Wouldn't you?"

She narrowed her eyes. "*Do* you have such information?"

"Absolutely," he lied, raking his memory for the name of any of his customers. Who had he seen recently? He tried to picture their faces, tried to see the paperwork he'd handled for them that very morning, but not a single one of their names came to him.

"What's your employee reference number?" she asked.

"329-84777," Jack replied.

She opened a deep drawer under her desk, and rifled through some files. "*Three* two nine?"

"That's right." Jack's mind worked furiously as he struggled to remember one—just one—of his customer's surnames. The old lady who'd dropped through the trapdoor yesterday? She had been… Miss Angelina *Clarin? Karen? Ka…*

"There's nothing here," the desk clerk said.

"I've worked here for seven months," Jack replied. *Keira? Clarion? Carlion? Carey? Clappy? Clarkson? Clarence? Clarin? Cle…? Cla…? Cli…? Clarina? Clamidia? Clipper? Claridma? Clint? Claw? Clawrin? Carin?*

"Carin," he said. "Miss Angelina Carin."

"I'm sorry, Mr Aviso," the desk clerk insisted. "We have no record of you ever having worked for us."

"Excuse me?"

"You're sure it was *three* two nine?"

"Of course I am. It's on every one of my payslips."

"There's no such number in the files."

Jack reached for his back pocket automatically. But then he realised he didn't have a payslip on him. They would all be in the box on the dresser back in Highcliffe, and he wasn't due to receive another one until the end of the month. *Could* he have been mistaken about the number? No, that was impossible. The second part pleased him because it was divisible by three, and the first part vaguely irked him because it wasn't. Initially, he'd asked Carol if she thought they'd change it to correct this discrepancy, but she'd only looked at him in the odd way that people sometimes do. "Can't you look under Aviso?"

"Not without the employee reference. It's company policy not to divulge—"

A buzzing sound came from the clock on the wall.

The desk clerk glanced up at it, then turned back to the customer who had been waiting patiently before her all of this time. "I'm afraid we are out of time, Mr Drummond," she said. "Please send in the next customer on your way out."

"But what about my appointment?" he replied.

She pushed a sheet of paper towards him across the desk. "You'll need to get a new reference from Complaints now."

"I have to queue up all over again?"

She shrugged.

The man stood up and glared at Jack. Then he snatched the document from the desk and walked away, red-faced and muttering to himself.

Jack barely noticed him go. He was looking at the two doors behind the desk.

"I'll have to ask you to leave, Mr Aviso."

"May I ask your name?" he said.

"I can't tell you that. It is against company policy for an employee to divulge any personal information without prior approval. "

"I thought as much," Jack muttered. He took out his handkerchief again, then strode around the desk and pulled the handle of the leftmost door. It was locked. He began trying different combinations. 999, 998, 997, 996…

"Mr Aviso?"

He gave up and marched over to the second door.

"I'm going to ring for Security."

The second door was also locked. He was about to roll the wheels to try a further combination, when alarm bells began to ring out from somewhere behind it. He turned back to the woman, and noticed that she had her foot firmly planted on a small pedal set in the floor. It had been hidden by the desk. Her cigarette moved in viscous little sweeps.

He hurried back outside.

The spokes of the Complaint Wheel fractured the cliff face above him, splitting the grey-brown rock into countless triangles and trapezoids. Steel and window glass glinted in the sunshine. He turned his back on the sight, gazing up instead at the main administration building. Its uniform façade gave no indications of the horrors said to be perpetrated within. Both staff and clients entered by the front doors, but clients didn't necessarily leave that way.

He turned away, then hesitated, and turned back. And then he began to jog along the front of the building, peering into every window he passed. Most of the ground floor appeared to contain small offices no larger than prison cells. Men and women hunched over desks, shifting paperwork from one pile to another. From each wall hung an identical clock—a simple white circle embossed with black numerals. Most of the clocks displayed thirteen minutes past four, but one of them indicted nine minutes past. He stopped and stared at this one for a long moment, his annoyance building. And then he started to run, passing room after room, cell after cell. He couldn't see his wife in any of them. When he reached the corner, he turned it and ran straight into two men.

These new arrivals both wore dark suits and pudding bowl hats. Jack recognised them at once: the stout, older man and the younger companion who had taken Carol from the Complaint Wheel less than ten minutes ago. He stopped, breathless, and opened his mouth to speak.

"Can we help you?" the younger man said.

"I'm looking for my wife," Jack replied. "You took her off the Wheel."

The two men exchanged a glance. The young man said, "What's your name?"

"Jack Aviso. My wife is Carol. Listen…" Jack spread his hands. "There's been some sort of mistake. If you let me speak to someone in charge, I'm sure I can sort this out."

"Carol Aviso?"

"That's right."

The older man looked back up at the Complaint Wheel. His young companion said, "I'm afraid you're mistaken, Mr Adams. We haven't taken anyone by that name from the wheel."

"Yes you did," Jack said. "I saw you."

"No," he said. "You didn't."

Now the elder of the two suits scrutinised Jack. "Shouldn't you be at work, Mr Adams?"

"Aviso. My name is Aviso."

The older man took a step forward. "I think we'd better escort you back to work."

Jack stepped back. "I'm not going anywhere with you."

"Be reasonable, Mr Adams," said the younger of the two.

"My name," Jack said, "is not Adams."

The older man grinned. He reached inside his jacket and withdrew a blackjack. "Just do me a favour," he said.

Jack eyed the weapon. "What?"

"Don't run."

Jack ran. He raced back the way he had come, past the queue outside the administration building, skidding round the corner and pounding down the stairs leading to the horse and carriage rank. Not once did he look behind him. When he reached the first of the carriages, he forced his way to the front of the line of waiting passengers, leapt up into the empty seat, and screamed at the driver to go. And only then did he realise that the Reclamation Men were nowhere to be seen.

The late afternoon sunlight slanted into Lower Cog town, drawing people out of the houses and tenement blocks and into the streams of commerce surrounding the water's edge. Fishermen crowded the pontoons along the banks of the Sill. Stallholders roasted sardines over charcoal in iron *kutas* or sold gold and silver, cloth, spices, leather and carved wooden god figurines brought from Alipo, Desulore and beyond. A group of priests from the Temple of Rys sat under the shade of a fig tree and read from their texts, while old men stood listening nearby and young children ran around shrieking and hurling fruit into the water. The air smelled of spices and river mud.

Jack kept his head low as the carriage crossed the Port Ellen Bridge and rattled into the avenues of Cog Island, skirting the old market square with its pastel hotel façades and its bridal lace cathedral. Henry Sill himself lived in the penthouse suite of the finest hotel of them all, sharing the entire building with nobody but a few trusted servants, and—it was rumoured—the desiccated corpses of his parents.

The driver left the island via Theatre Bridge, and zigzagged up the lanes into Highcliffe. Carol's family had deep roots here. Her grandfather, Hans, had been a successful playwright in his time, her grandmother, Julia, a respected actress. In twenty years they had amassed the fortune Carol's father would subsequently squander producing his lavish and wildly unpopular theatrical polemics. Their former town house on Gibbald Street now belonged to Mr Sill's bank, while Jack and his wife lived in an airy white-washed old apartment on Oldrum Place that she had inherited from her twitchy, one-armed aunt.

Jack considered himself lucky. Had they not owned their home outright, their combined wages would have confined them to Port Sellen or one of the other fish-roasting districts. *Here, at least,* he thought, as the driver reined in outside the front door of Jack's building, *one has the space and grandeur in which to unwind.*

A coil of marble steps took him up to the third floor landing. But when he tried his key in his own apartment's door, the lock wouldn't turn. He struggled with it for a while before giving up and beating his handkerchief upon the wood. "Carol?" he called. "Are you there? It's me."

A moment later, he heard—to his great relief—the sound of footsteps inside the apartment. The lock clicked, and the door opened.

"You won't believe—"

Jack stopped. Standing there, inside his apartment, was a heavyset man wearing a dressing gown. His soiled white nightshirt constrained an ample paunch that ballooned out over the outer garment's cord. His jaw was unshaven, his long brown hair all knotted and tussled, and his eyes still bleary from sleep.

Jack said, "Who are you?"

The stranger's eyes focused on him, and his jaw moved back and forwards in a somewhat bovine manner. A frown creased his brow. "What do you want?" he said.

"What are you doing in my apartment? Where's my wife?"

The intruder frowned at Jack a moment longer, and then a light of comprehension seemed to come into his eyes. "Are you him?" he said.

"Who?"

The intruder's expression locked up again. "I don't have anything to say to you. You're not supposed to be here."

"Where's Carol?"

He went to close the door, but Jack pushed against it.

The pair of them struggled. "I bought this place fair and square," the intruder said. "Fair and square."

"*Where is my wife?*"

"I don't know!" With one final colossal heave, he managed to slam the door in Jack's face.

Jack beat his fist against the wood to no avail. Using his handkerchief, he pushed the letterbox open and peered in to see that huge dressing gown hurrying away down the hall. The narrow space still contained the bookcase Carol had painted with daisies, and the rug they'd purchased at the Lammerday market last year. The sight of these things only renewed his frustration. He raised his fist, and was about to hammer on the door again, when he heard a voice from behind.

"We told you not to run, Mr Adams."

Jack turned to see the same two men in pudding bowl hats he'd encountered earlier, now standing a short distance down the stairway. They climbed the remaining steps to join him on the landing.

The younger of the two smiled in a condescending manner. "I am Mr Younger," he said, then gestured towards his companion. "And this is Mr Elder. He doesn't like to run after people."

"Too old for it," Elder said.

"Where is she?" Jack asked.

Younger shrugged. "That's not for me to say, Mr Adams."

"My name is Aviso."

Younger shook his head. "Not any longer, Mr Adams." He reached inside his suit pocket, took out a folded sheet of paper, and handed it to Jack. "The Henry Sill Banking Corporation has been forced to alter your circumstances in order to reclaim debts owed to them."

"What debts?"

"The document in your possession is a sale receipt," Younger said. "It pertains to your property at 113 Skiptag Road, Knuckletown."

Jack scanned the document. He could see that it did, indeed, relate to a sale by auction—this very afternoon—of someone else's house, but he couldn't have cared less. "This isn't mine," he said. "I've never owned property in Knuckletown. I don't even know where Skiptag Road is."

"That isn't significant," Younger said. "What is significant is that we have been authorised to reclaim the outstanding balance." He peered over the top of the paper in Jack's hand. "From a Mr Cotton Adams of—"

"I told you, my name is not—"

Elder broke in, his voice booming: "Your name is Adams. You live at—*lived at*—113 Skiptag Road, Knuckletown, and you owe us"—he glanced at the palm of his hand—"11,024 ducats and change." He leaned closer, until his nostrils almost touched Jack's cheek. "And you *will* settle this account one way or another."

Jack looked from Younger to Elder. His heart was fluttering in his chest, and now all the strength had drained from his legs. If he managed to shove the two men aside, would he even be able to run down the stairs and get away? And to what end? It wouldn't help him locate Carol. "Please," he said, "just take me to my wife. We'll work something out. I'll do whatever you ask."

The two Reclamation Men exchanged a glance. Some unspoken communication seemed to pass between them. Finally, Younger said, "I'm afraid we can't do that."

Elder grinned. "Mr Adams never married."

His hand seized Jack's arm.

Jack lashed out instinctively, overcome with feelings of fear and revulsion. He tried desperately to shake the Reclamation man off, but throughout their tussle Elder maintained an unbreakable grip on his jacket sleeve. His fear became terror. Howling, he struck out blindly with his other fist and punched the Reclamation man in the face. And then his shoe slipped on the marble floor. He stumbled sideways; his shoulder slammed into the wall. Elder must have lost his hold on him because suddenly Jack was free. He ran.

He clattered down the stairs, deaf to the sound of everything but his own thumping blood and heaving lungs. One landing, two landings, and then he reached the front door and burst through it and took off, the soles of his shoes slapping the cobbled road with a sound like applause.

The light spilling from Marley's living room window illuminated a skewed tombstone of pavement. Jack watched the street from the shadows of an alleyway opposite. He was still shaking. All seemed quiet. Even here, two streets back from the shore, he could smell the Sill River mud. He had spied a dark shape—what he imagined to be a figure, crouching under a shop canopy further down the road—but it hadn't moved an inch in all the time he'd waited here.

Just a shadow.

He had heard voices, too—shouts and barks of laughter coming from a nearby street, but they'd moved away in the direction of the harbour.

Just drunks.

Jack shoved his hands in his pockets, crossed the street, and rang Marley's bell.

He waited, listening for that sudden cry, the pounding of boots on the road behind him. But nothing happened.

Marley opened the door. "Jack?"

"Can I come in?"

Marley hesitated. He glanced up and down the street. "What are you doing here?"

"I don't know where else to go."

The old timer cast his eyes up and down the street once more, then beckoned Jack inside.

"You think the same thing happened to Carol?"

Marley nodded. "She'll have a new name, a new job, and new lodgings by now."

They had taken refuge in two of the three padded chairs before the old timer's fire. He'd closed the drapes and turned the oil lamp down. The room smelled of horsehair furniture and old carpet, mingled with a bitter hint of tea. A glass-domed clock on the mantle ticked away the moments while its silvery innards span like the vanes of an anemometer. Jack sat on his handkerchief and warmed his hands on his mug while he listened.

"They call it a Citizen Record Adjustment," Marley went on. "Whenever a debtor dies or absconds, and Reclamation can't recover enough from his assets, the bank has no legal right to transfer his debt on to someone else. However, under certain circumstances they *do* have the right to amend the citizen records and the land registry up at Cavendish Hall—typically in cases of suspected fraud. The bank will have claimed that this Mr Adams tried to escape his debts by assuming a new identity." He pointed at Jack. "They then provide a summary of their investigations to the court—investigations which are never undertaken, I might add. One of Sill's lawmakers then rubber stamps the transferral orders, and Reclamation takes over."

Jack shook his head. "I didn't think the courts would ever stoop this low."

"Well, Henry Sill owns the courts," Marley said.

"But why hasn't there been an outcry?"

Marley sighed. "There was. You probably didn't hear about it. Few people ever do. Look, the problem you face is trying to prove that you are who you claim to be, when the records clearly state otherwise."

"We have friends, people who can vouch for us."

"The court won't hear them," Marley said. "In their eyes you're a fraudster. They're not going to listen to anyone you summon in order to support that fraud. This isn't about who is right, Jack. It's about profit."

"Why me? Why us?"

The old man shrugged. "It could just be bad luck. You and Carol owned your apartment outright, but you don't have any children to inherit it. When the bank adjusted your records, they effectively wiped you out. You don't legally exist. The property then goes to so-called public auction, which isn't really public because it's not announced. The bank buys it at a fraction of its worth and sells it on to someone else, usually one of their debtors." He took a sip of tea. "The whole thing can take less than an hour if the paperwork is already in place."

"They were selling my house this morning? While I sat in that wheel and worked for them?"

Marley nodded. "Looks that way. Did you do anything to aggravate them?"

Jack hesitated. "Carol resolved a complaint."

"A debt?"

"I don't know."

"Nothing else?"

Jack shook his head.

Marley leaned forward in his chair, picked up a log, and tossed it into the fire. "It's unusual for them to target their own employees," he said. "But it does happen. And once they cut you out of the fold, there's no getting back in again. Do you have any money tucked away?"

"About 400. It was hidden in the apartment."

"Then it's gone. I'm afraid this is going to be a difficult time for both of you."

Jack clutched his mug. "How do I find her, Marley?"

Marley drained his own drink and then put it down beside the fire. "People like Henry Sill possess a very deep and profound sense of entitlement, Jack. They don't see people like us as anything more than barriers to wealth that ought to be theirs by rights. And the more wealth they accumulate, the more that feeling is compounded. They are the gods' chosen few. Carol means absolutely nothing to him. But I'll tell you this…if you find her, and if you try to take her out of whatever hole he's put her in, he'll react with just as much fury and moral indignation as if you'd kidnapped one of his own children."

"He has children?" Jack said.

Marley shrugged.

Jack got up from his seat. "So where do I look for her? Where do I even begin?"

The old man gazed into the fire. "There are rumours," he said. "But you're not going to like it, Jack."

"What do you mean?"

"Reclamation puts most of the men to work in the mines," Marley said. "It's *possible* they put her there, too."

"But you don't think so?"

He picked up the poker and jabbed at the fire. "Carol is a bright and attractive young lady," he said. "And Henry Sill owns a number of establishments where feminine charms are in demand."

Jack felt his gut tighten.

"Down by the harbour," Marley said. "Or, so I'm told."

DOWN BY THE HARBOUR,
OR SO I'M TOLD

ALINE OF TUMBLEDOWN HOUSES stood ten yards back from the water's edge, their windows ablaze with colourful paper lanterns and candles that spilled fans of light across the wharf. Music and laughter came from within each place, producing a riotous cacophony that drifted out over the dark quiet shapes of the battleships moored in the harbour.

Jack waited under the shadow of one of these metal hulks. He had been here for ten minutes already. A couple of lights shone above him, marking the place where a steep gangplank connected with the hull, but the decks and bridge all seemed devoid of life. The sailors were making the best of their shore leave.

He returned his attention to the brothels. There were six of them, and he did not know where to start. All appeared to be as raucous and unwelcoming as the next. Was he expected to pay at the door? He reached into his pocket, and counted out a meagre three ducats in coins. Jack shoved the change back into his pocket, tugged his suit jacket collar tighter around his neck, and walked towards the lights.

He chose a door with a green lantern shining above, and stepped inside.

A wave of heat and noise engulfed him. He found himself in a richly decorated lounge packed from golden drape to tasselled curtain with a whole battalion of rough and ugly sorts. Woman draped themselves over sailors reclining on garish couches, or shrieked and giggled and spilled wine, while hands reached inside bodices and fumbled under skirts. Groups of men clustered around the bar, where a small hook-nosed man in a white shirt worked endlessly pouring spirits into ranks of shot glasses. In one corner, a red-faced man tortured a squeeze box, while his spidery companion plucked at the strings of a long-necked mandolier. A pall of cigarette smoke hung in the air at shoulder level, having already passed innumerable times through the lungs of the sailors and their whores. The carpet clung momentarily to the sole of Jack's shoe when he took a step, releasing him as a wound releases a bandage.

Jack stood there, confounded by this whirlwind of sweating bodies, until a young woman staggered over and flopped her hot, damp arms around his neck. She raised her chin and breathed up at him with practised sultriness, albeit tempered by a veneer of boredom. "You want to buy me a drink?" she said. Her breath smelled of liquor and marzipan.

He disentangled himself. "I'm looking for my wife."

"A wife?"

"*My* wife," he said. "Her name is Carol Aviso."

Her interest in him evaporated; her gaze moved off in search of other clients.

"Do you know her?"

"Unlikely," she said, wandering off.

Jack made his way across to the bar, and squeezed into a space between two groups of sailors. The bartender continued filling shot glasses, and didn't glance up. Hundreds of bottles cluttered the wall behind, their labels screaming countless unlikely proclamations. A narrow-shouldered man to Jack's left turned his back on his companions, and regarded Jack with bleary eyes.

"Bank worker," he said.

Jack ignored him.

"You are a bank worker," the sailor repeated.

Jack glanced his way, then returned his attention to the barman.

"Am I right?"

Jack looked back at the sailor. "I was."

"I knew it. I can always tell people. It's like..." His gaze slurred all over Jack's suit jacket. "You know..? I can always tell."

Jack nodded.

"She's like the Port Road," the sailor said.

The barman was *still* busy pouring drinks, taking money from people, putting it in a leather pouch on his belt. He hadn't even bothered to acknowledge Jack's presence.

"More traffic, in and out," the sailor said. "You know what I mean?" He grinned and lifted a fist. "The Port Road."

"Who is?"

"The girl," the sailor said.

"What girl?"

The other man frowned. "What do you mean, *what girl*? The girl, man. *The girl.*"

Jack just nodded again.

"So what do you think about that?" the sailor asked.

"About what?"

"The Port Road."

"I don't know what you mean," Jack replied.

The sailor screwed up his face with frustration. "Avelina," he said. "That's what I'm saying." He raised his glass to his lips before noticing it was empty, then gazed at it suspiciously, as if trying to determine how this could possibly have happened. He pulled out a fistful of coins from his pocket, spilling most of them across the floor, then stooped to pick them up, wavering like an invalid on the very brink of death.

Jack began to suspect that the barman was deliberately ignoring him. "Excuse me," he said.

The barman didn't turn round, but took an order from another customer instead.

The sailor next to Jack had by now gathered up a handful of coins. He tipped them onto the bar beside his empty glass. "Bank worker," he drawled. "You know how I know that?"

"The suit," Jack said.

"That's right."

Jack wasn't getting anywhere with the barman. He turned to the sailor. "Do all the girls in here work for Mr Sill?" he asked.

The sailor thought about this for a long time. Eventually, he said, "I think they work for Mr Sill."

"What about new girls?"

The other man nodded. "Sometimes," he said, "but not all the time."

"Where do they bring the new girls?"

"To the boat," he said.

"What boat?"

"Have you got any money?"

"What boat?"

"In the harbour. "

"There's a boat in the harbour where they bring the new girls?"

"Of course there's a boat," the sailor said. "Why isn't there?"

"Where is the boat?"

The man waved his hand in a lilting manner. "In the harbour."

Away from the bordello lanterns, moonlight picked out lines of shipsteel and cable in the darkness. Silver flecks danced upon the water, stretching out towards the seaward harbour wall. Jack hurried along the wharf, searching for a sign of revelry—music or lights—among the great naval shadows, but the warships each crouched in their own vast swathes of gloom. Destroyers and cruisers hunched against the dock like sleeping giants, while fat black pipes hummed oil into their engine rooms. From here to the end of the wharf, Jack could see that the remaining ships were all military vessels, and thus unlikely candidates for his search. He turned back to search in the opposite direction, and ran straight into a young woman.

Her manner of clothing suggested she had come from one of the bordellos, although Jack couldn't recall seeing her in the place he'd visited. She was rakishly thin, but pretty, and carried herself in the stooped and brittle fashion of someone always ready to flinch. A minor disfigurement marked her lip, perhaps a burn or a scar that had tightened the skin and raised one side of her mouth, giving her the merest suggestion of a sneer.

"I didn't want to shout," the woman said, "but you just kept on walking. I'm not supposed to be out here."

Jack looked at her. "You know something about my wife?"

She hesitated. "Maybe. Did she come from the wheel?"

He nodded.

"What did she look like?"

"About your height, but fair. She was wearing a grey jacket—"

"No," the woman cut in. "They dress them all before they bring them down here. You won't find Sill's boat, anyway. It's out at sea now."

The news tightened itself around Jack's stomach.

"But something happened today," the woman said. "You need to know about that." She glanced back along the wharf in the direction of the bordellos. "One of the girls tried to run," she said, "and two of Sill's men went for her. There was a scuffle. I don't think they meant to hurt her, but…" She hesitated. "There was an accident. She hit her head, and…"

"Where?"

"She hit her head *really* bad. I can show you where they left the body."

Jack's blood drained from his limbs, leaving him suddenly weak and numb.

"I don't know if it's her," the woman said.

"What did she look like?"

She hesitated. "Fair, like you said."

The woman led Jack back the way he had come, past the row of bordellos with their bright paper lanterns, towards the southern end of the harbour. She said her name was Eloise and she'd seen it all from her window. Two of Sill's men had taken four girls to the boat, but one was crying and refused to board. They'd struck her, and she'd tried to run. One of the men captured the screaming girl and threw her to the ground. But she'd fallen hard, and cracked her head against the corner of a concrete block, the base of one of the loading cranes. She hadn't got up again, and the man had kicked her in the stomach before the other one shouted at him to stop. There had been blood on her face, but not much. Some of the girls had come out from one of the bordellos to help, but they'd been ordered to go back. And then the port constable had appeared and he helped Mr Sill's men carry the stricken woman up the gangplank and onto the boat. They took her below decks, and when they carried her back out again ten minutes later, she'd still wasn't moving. The port constable had watched while Mr Sill's men threw her body into the harbour.

Jack listened to all of this while a thousand different thoughts reeled through his head. He tried to convince himself that this woman couldn't have been Carol, that the Reclamation Men he'd met earlier would have made some comment if this had indeed been the case, but he couldn't quell the clawing sense of dread. Eloise fell silent as they approached a quieter part of the harbour, where three wooden jetties struck out from the main wharf underneath the southern breakwater. Half a dozen yachts lay moored in the darkness. She led him down some steps onto the third jetty, then squatted down by the water's edge and pointed.

"There."

Jack peered into the gloom between the yachts. Water gurgled and slapped the jetty pillars under his feet. At first he couldn't see anything. But then he spotted an indistinct shape floating four yards out from the shore.

He jumped in.

Cold seawater crashed over his head, tightened around his chest. He broke the surface, gasping, then swam over towards the body—for there was no longer any doubt in his mind that that was what it was. She was wearing a light summer dress that had partially distended, jellyfish-like, above her shoulders. Her hair drifted like a mat of weed, bobbing in the waves. Her pale arms floated just below the surface of the water.

Jack rolled his wife over and looked into her lifeless eyes.

MEETING MR HENRY SILL

AFTERWARDS, HE WOULD BARELY remember how he managed to drag her from the water. By the time he finally pulled his wife's body onto the jetty, Eloise had disappeared. He recalled sitting beside Carol for a long time, shivering and sobbing, while the music and laughter from the bordellos drifted out into the night.

He hadn't wanted to leave her there, but she had been too heavy for him to carry. At some point, he had decided to return to Marley's house for help, but he had no recollection of that particular journey at all.

Marley had handed him a glass of frighteningly strong liqueur, and then sat grimly on his chair beside the fire while Jack wept and convulsed. The old timer hadn't said very much, but his eyes had been full of grave concern. He'd offered Jack a change of clothes, but Jack refused.

"Do you think she's in hell?" Jack said.

"I don't know, Jack. The Priests of Rys might be able to tell you."

"I can't just leave her body lying there."

Marley swallowed his drink, winced, and reached for the bottle. "We could bring her here," he said, "but by rights it ought to be a matter for the port constable."

"The constable *watched* them dump her," Jack said.

Marley was silent for a long time. Jack could see the mechanism of his mind working behind those tired old eyes. Finally the old man stood up and said, "Let me see what I can do." He went upstairs, and when he returned he had on a long woollen coat and a dark cloth cap. "You'd better stay here," he said. "I'll speak to the constable alone."

He was gone for over an hour. Jack waited in the old man's front room and listened to the tick of the mantle clock and the crackle of coal in the hearth. He drank and he thought about Carol: sitting on their couch in Highcliffe, tying knots in his socks while he tried to read the application form she'd brought back from the bank. He remembered the picnic they'd taken in Alderney, where he'd asked her to marry him, the square blue sheet laid out on the grass, the smell of the wine, her happy bemusement turning to concern over his terror of wasps. The day they'd carried their furniture up the stairs to their apartment, the sweat on her brow as she struggled with the lower end of the dresser, the red headscarf she's been wearing. The way she'd drink from a mug still stained with grime without washing it first. He thought about their wedding, their small reception in the Gold Theatre parlour. Carol's friends Anne and Mar had been there; George and Beth, too; Aunt Jem and the pair from Unta; some actor and his girlfriend; all reeling to the Horse Race and the Captain's Lead Lady and other dances from Brome and Caldera while someone's children ran about and shrieked—a whirling of faces he hadn't really cared about or wanted to see again. He'd been drunk then and it occurred to him that he was getting drunk now. He took great gulps of Marley's foul liqueur, savouring the burning in his throat. It felt like anger. And ultimately his thoughts returned to the incident this morning: His wife's shoes slipping on the rocky ground as the Reclamation Men took her away.

It was after midnight when Marley returned. The old man looked weary as he took off his cap and jacket and dumped them over the back of a chair. "They've taken her to the mortuary," he said. "I'll make arrangements for the funeral tomorrow." He sat down and gave a heavy sigh. "You won't be able to attend that, Jack."

"The constable's men took her to the mortuary?"

Marley nodded.

"How much did it cost you?"

Marley reached for the bottle, but stopped when he noticed it was empty. He shrugged. "Little enough. I don't want you worrying about that."

Jack stared at his own empty glass. "Will you help me do something, Marley?"

"What?"

"Help me kill Henry Sill."

Marley sighed again. "No, Jack. I won't. You should get some sleep."

Jack didn't sleep well. He lay on Marley's couch, drifting in and out of nightmares in which the Reclamation Men led Carol through the streets of Cog City. They were always turning the next corner, and no matter how hard he ran after them he could never catch up. He woke up to find his stomach bucking, and ran to retch into the kitchen sink.

He splashed water over his face and gazed out of the window. Marley's kitchen overlooked a tiny courtyard, a stone cell trapped between the surrounding tenement blocks. The windowsills and drainpipes existed as ill-defined grey shapes in the pre-dawn gloom. Someone had set out clay pots packed with soil, but there was nothing growing there yet. Jack opened the drawer next to the sink and took out the largest of Marley's kitchen knives. He cleaned the blade carefully under the running tap, and dried it with his handkerchief, before slipping it into his jacket pocket.

He left the apartment before Marley got up, stepping out into the chill morning mist that always pooled in the streets down by the shore. He felt wretched, woollen headed, and yet still driven by the same bleak determination that had haunted his dreams. Few people were about at this hour: a couple of market traders carrying rolls of canvas and poles in the direction of the river; a street cleaner following a pail cart with his broom.

By the time Jack reached Cog Island the restaurateurs and tea vendors were already setting up in the old market square, wiping dew from the chairs clustered outside their establishments, flopping down cushions, and erecting parasols over the tables. The cathedral occupied one entire side of the square, its white spires and bell tower towering over the pastel façades of the other buildings. Henry Sill lived in the Margareta Hotel directly opposite—a great pink cake of a building with white icing window frames. It had been named after the pirate ship that had brought his ancestor here.

Jack walked through the main door of the hotel and into the foyer.

Reflections from a score of golden chandeliers and floor-standing candelabras glimmered in the green marble walls, imbuing the chamber with a faintly subaquatic ambience. Directly opposite the main entrance, a staircase snaked around the ironwork of an old cage elevator. A counter of dark wood enclosed the former reception area to Jack's left, where hundreds of keys still glittered on their wall pegs. As Jack wandered across the polished floor, the man behind reception looked up with an expression of alarm. He was thin and bent, with a pencil line moustache and a veneer of glossy black hair.

"We are not open to the public," he said.

Jack walked towards the elevator.

"Excuse me?" the man said, coming around the counter. "You can't go there."

Jack took out his handkerchief and used it to pull the cage door open, and then slam it closed behind him again. He glanced at the array of numbered buttons. Sill lived in the penthouse. Jack pressed the uppermost button.

And nothing happened.

He jabbed the button again, but still the elevator didn't move. And then he noticed a small, but elaborately decorated brass and ivory keypad underneath the larger, floor selection buttons. It consisted of nine numbers arrayed in groups of three, and a tenth button underneath marked *reset*. Evidently this was some sort of security device. The elevator could not be operated without first typing in the correct code.

Jack hissed through his teeth.

The receptionist had been hurrying across the floor. Now he stopped and ran back towards his desk. "Stay where you are," he cried over his shoulder. "I'm calling security."

Jack studied the keypad. Nine numbers. He doubted the combination would be longer than three or four digits, but that still meant that it could be any sequence of numbers between 111 and 9999, and he didn't have time to try them all. What numbers would Henry Sill have chosen? Jack typed 123, then hit the top floor button again.

Nothing.

He hit the rest button, and tried 1234.

Nothing.

111.

Nothing.

999.

Nothing.

Jack clenched his hands his frustration. He had to *think*. Henry Sill had been living in this hotel for nearly thirty years. He would have used this elevator countless times, which meant he would have typed in the code countless times. There was no other way to operate the thing. Jack crouched and examined the keypad closely, looking for signs of wear. Of all the nine buttons, only the one marked '5' appeared to be significantly more worn than the others. The ivory looked a little more yellowed, the ink a little more scratched.

He typed in 555.

Somewhere above, the mechanism clunked into life. The elevator jerked once, and began to rise.

Alarm bells began to sound.

The elevator shuddered upwards in a great clamour of rattling iron, passing landings where the staircase joined identical corridors of numbered doors. After six floors the landings stopped, but the elevator continued its ascent through a narrow wood-walled shaft. He could still hear the alarms, now muted, coming from below. The elevator slowed, then, with a final wheeze and a clunk, came to a stop before a large, bright antechamber.

Jack stepped out onto a glassy floor. Archways on either side of him opened into luxurious chambers. Through the right-most opening he spied the edge of a four poster bed shrouded in gauzy drapes. The opposite chamber, to his left, looked more like a parlour, so he wandered over to the entrance of this room and peered inside. The sound of the alarms was much quieter here, and he could hear something else: a regular clacking, as if somebody nearby was using a typewriter.

Morning flooded in through tall windows overlooking the market square. It gleamed on enamelled lamp bases and bone-pale ceramic vases, and burst through the prisms of an enormous crystal chandelier, scattering rainbows across the many portraits adorning the walls. These were gilt framed images of old men in archaic clothing, presumably Henry Sill's ancestors. Chairs and couches of vermilion and cinnabar silk had been artfully positioned around low tables carved from onyx or blood-coloured wood or wrought entirely from gold. The floor reflected everything above it like a still pool. The chamber was empty. Jack realised the clacking sound was coming from the room across the hall.

The bedroom was as opulent as the lounge, rich in plum and raspberry silks and great sparkling mounds of gold cushions. A riotous expanse of floral paper covered the back wall.

Constellations of gemstones studded the ceiling. The strange sound appeared to be emanating from the huge, gauze-entombed bed, behind whose drapes Jack could just perceive the form of a reclining figure. He slipped Marley's kitchen knife out of his pocket. Then he walked over to the bed and used the blade to peel back the drapes.

He stifled a cry.

Lying before him was the desiccated corpse of Henry Sill. The face, flung back in a rictus of death, stared up with sightless eye sockets. The skin had turned leathery and grey, and receded around the mouth, giving the visage a hideous, yellow-toothed grimace. The corpse had been dressed in a dusty old suit, and evidently treated with some chemical preservative. Jack covered his nose at the stench of it. But whoever had done this had not been content to simply retard the process of decay, for the body itself had been altered in a ghastly fashion.

Henry Sill's hands had been removed entirely.

As if to compensate for this bizarre amputation, two empty leather gloves lay flat against the bed sheet. The clacking noise was much louder here. It seemed to be coming from the head of the bed. As Jack let the drapes fall back, he let his gaze wander towards the sound. And there he spied a small door in the wall nearby. It had been camouflaged with floral paper and wainscoting to resemble part of the wall itself.

Jack took out his handkerchief again.

The door led to a windowless chamber no larger than a closet. It was empty but for a darkly gleaming contraption set against the far wall. The machine consisted of a complex nest of interwoven glass tubes, each full of crimson fluid. These vessels appeared to both originate from and terminate at a central sphere, itself transparent and full of the same liquid. Beneath this lay an enormous roll of paper confined within a brass spool. Every few moments the spool would suddenly give a *click*, and turn fractionally around on its axle. And yet the source of the rapid clacking noise remained a mystery. The closet contained no typewriter, nor any parts moving quickly enough to account for the sound he heard. Jack walked up to the machine and examined it more closely. To his astonishment, he noticed that words were materialising on the roll of paper, one letter at a time, as though at the hands of an invisible typist. He started to read.

Increase tertiary interest by 0.3%, add accumulated change to quaternary in the second term, all savings accounts to be modified to incorporate hosting fees of nine guilders per annum, hosting fees to purchase shares in potentially loss-making business ventures, transferring risk to account holders, any profit from such shares must of course remain inaccessible to account holders—recommend funnelling through secondary high maintenance account using normal...

"Good morning, Mr Adams."

Jack turned to find Mr Younger and Mr Elder standing in the room behind him.

Elder turned to Younger. "He's carrying a knife, Mr Younger. Do you suppose he intended to harm Mr Sill?"

"I imagine so," Younger said. He grinned at Jack. "You are sixteen months too late, Mr Adams. Mr Sill, as you can see, is no longer with us in the flesh."

"He left this world to pursue a business venture in Hell," Elder said.

Younger nodded. "The company is expanding."

Jack gripped his knife and backed away as Elder sidled past him. The reclamation man stopped before the machine, and peered down at the spool of paper. "Fortunately for all of us, Mr Sill still maintains a tight rein on all his business operations back here. I see he's raising interest rates again."

"That's rather unfortunate for Mr Adams."

"But good for the bank," Elder said.

"Very good for the bank," Younger agreed.

Younger was blocking Jack's exit, while Elder now stood behind him. Jack flattened himself against the wall, but he couldn't keep the knife pointed at both reclamation men simultaneously.

"We expected to find you here eventually," Elder said.

"But not quite so soon," Younger added. "It's fair to say you didn't strike us as a particularly driven man. More of a planner than a doer, wouldn't you say, Mr Elder?"

"Definitely a planner, Mr Younger."

Jack said, "Were you at the harbour?"

Younger seemed to lose the arrogance from his expression for just an instant, but then it was back again. "The matter of your outstanding debt remains unresolved, Mr Adams. The courts have now authorised us to escort you to one of Mr Sill's mines, where you will be given employment at a diminished wage until—"

"*Were you at the harbour?*"

The two Reclamation Men exchanged a glance. Younger said, "Where you will be given employment at a diminished wage until such time as the outstanding sum is repaid in full."

Jack's rage exploded. He screamed and rushed at the man, hacking madly at the air with his knife. Younger recoiled, with an expression of disbelief on his face, as the blade plunged towards his shoulder. Jack felt the steel connect with flesh and then bone. He jerked it out and stabbed a second time, and a third, until his vision filled with blood.

Elder seized him from behind.

Jack wrenched his body around, striking out with the knife again. He heard a wheeze as it punctured Elder's side. The man's grip slackened. And then Jack was running, still screaming, slipping across the floor and through the arch and out into the antechamber.

He stumble inside the elevator cage door, and slammed it shut after him.

He jabbed the lowest button with bloody fingers, but nothing happened.

Jack screamed again, hammering his finger against the keypad.

555

This time the cage began to descend. As he slumped back against the wall, shuddering with fear and fury, he caught a glimpse of Younger's boots in the antechamber above. And then the elevator had descended below the level of the floor and was plunging ever deeper into that narrow shaft.

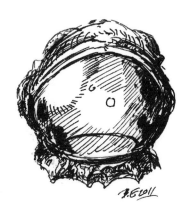

GOING DOWN

THE OTHER COMPLAINANTS WAITED patiently in the glare of the afternoon sun. Every few minutes they would shuffle forwards another step. The complaint form in Jack's hand hadn't come from the Document Office. The Document Office wouldn't have issued Jack with one because he didn't have an account. He still wanted to complain, however, and Marley had come to his rescue with some unofficial paperwork.

Good old Marley. Jack owed him so much, and he still felt pangs of regret that he would never be able to repay the old man. Carol's funeral had cost more than Jack could have earned in months, but Marley had footed the bill—finally finding a good use for all the trapdoor wagers he'd won over the years, or so he'd claimed.

Think of it as a present from everyone who ever hit the dirt, Jack.

And Marley had attended the ceremony in Jack's absence. He'd stood by her graveside and read a poem from Lovich's *The Burning Sail*, Carol's favourite play, and then he'd placed flowers upon the mound of earth while the Priest of Rys looked on.

Marley had given him Charles Rain's book, too, when he realised Jack could not be diverted from his plan. That had been two weeks ago, and he'd been memorising it furiously ever since.

Fear a stranger's knock upon your door, and you will immediately hear such a report, for he will be standing outside, and his intentions will be whatever you—in your worst nightmares—have imagined them to be.

Jack had shaved his hair down to the knuckle of his scalp. He'd already looped a noose around his neck, and hidden it under his shirt collar. The loose coils of rope he'd stuffed into his shirt gave him the appearance of a paunch.

The queue moved on another step.

"You know it's all a farce," said the elderly man waiting in the queue behind Jack. "They never resolve complaints, they just stamp your form and pass you on to Reclamation. My daughter, Lilly—"

"Then why bother coming here?" Jack said.

The man shrugged. "What choice do I have? You need to have *some* faith in human decency. Otherwise what's the point of struggling on?"

Jack made a gesture of non-committal. Henry Sill had no human decency. The dead banker was no longer human and yet no less human than he'd ever been.

He could see the embarkation platform and the top of the wheel now, the steward herding groups of complainants into the slowly rotating chambers, while the teeth of the ore processors chewed gold in the depths of the earth.

"Six to a cabin, quickly now."

Jack reached the platform. He had promised Marley not to use his friend's particular cabin, but now that he was here, he couldn't see how he was supposed to determine which one to avoid. He had little choice but to put his faith in the odds.

The steward barely glanced his way as he urged the group into the wheel's uppermost compartment. Boards crackled underfoot, and suddenly Jack found himself standing in the gloom on the opposite side of the grilles for the first time in his life. He cast his gaze around, and, to his overwhelming relief, did not spy Marley among the tellers on duty here. Recognising none of them, he chose one at random.

"Mr Aviso," the young man behind the grille said, reading Jack's complaint form. "I am obliged to inform you that we have about 90 seconds before this cabin reaches ground level, whereupon all customers must disembark. The Henry Sill Banking Corporation cannot be held liable for any injuries sustained by a customer who fails to disembark promptly."

Jack unbuttoned his shirt collar and glanced up at the lamp hook in the ceiling.

"Now, according to this…" The bank teller stopped, frowning. He read a little more, then cupped his chin in one hand. His tongue flicked out, lizard-like, and retreated. He looked to the man sitting next to him for assistance, only to find that that particular colleague was already busy with another customer. Finally, he returned his attention to the form. "I think there's been some mistake," he said.

"No mistake," Jack, unbuttoning his shirt.

The teller's frown remained fixed on the form. "But, it says here…"

"It says," Jack said, "that the Henry Sill Banking Corporation forced my wife into prostitution, murdered her, and then dumped her body in the harbour." Jack opened his shirt and the coils of rope tumble out. "That's what I want to complain about."

The teller's expression of bemusement turned to one of alarm, as he noticed the noose around Jack's neck

Jack reached up, fed the loose rope through the ceiling hook, and pulled it until it was taut. "Do I need a reference number?" he said.

"Excuse me?"

The clock on the wall chimed.

"Do I need a reference number to take my complaint further?" Jack said, wrapping the excess rope around the ceiling hook. The cabin grew quieter as the other tellers, and most of the customers, noticed what he was doing. Those few who had remained engaged in conversations fell silent a moment later. Everyone was staring at him.

"Um," the teller said.

The clock on the wall chimed again.

"What's the matter, lad?" This remark came from the elderly man who had been in the queue behind Jack. He stood nearby, his brow furrowed with concern.

Jack felt tears beginning to well in his eyes, and he bit down the urge to sob. His heart was racing now, his breaths coming quick and shallow. "I'm giving them the chance to resolve my complaint," he said evenly. He tugged on the rope to make sure it was fixed securely above him. The noose bit savagely into his neck.

"Whatever happened," the elderly man said, "it isn't worth this."

Jack gave him a grim smile. "I just want my complaint resolved," he said.

The elderly man turned to the teller. "Do it."

"Um," the teller said.

"Help him."

The teller spread his hands. "I don't know... I don't know how."

"I'll tell you how," Jack said to the teller. "I want every man and woman employed by this corporation to come in here *right now*, and kneel on the floor and beg for my dead wife's forgiveness." His voice started to falter. "And then I want Henry Sill's corpse dragged out into the sunlight and left to rot until I receive a message from The Lord of Hell himself telling me that the owner of this corporation has thrown his soul into a Mesmerist cesspit. And I want it done now, because if isn't, I'll go to Hell myself and spend the rest of *my* eternity making the rest of *his* eternity unbearable."

The clock began to chime repeatedly.

"Ten seconds," Jack said.

The teller opened his mouth.

The door to the disembarkation platform opened with a *thud* and a sudden inpouring of light. The customers fled, until only the silhouette of the elderly man lingered in the doorway. Then he, too, turned away. In a hoarse whisper he said, "You made that rope too taut, son."

Jack grinned manically. "Don't you get it?" he said. "This is—"

The trapdoor opened below him.

THE SUICIDE CLUB

ACCORDING TO CHARLES RAIN'S book, surviving Damnation depended almost entirely on one's ability to control one's mental state, and therefore one's environment. Since an individual's amount of personal space in Hell was largely determined by his confidence and sheer-bloody-minded aggression, it was all too easy for the Damned to give up in despair and allow themselves to be crushed by the minds around them.

Jack resolved to remain focused on his objective. He began to test the boundaries of his prison.

By determined concentration, he found that he was able, after a while, to enlarge the room he occupied by several square feet. He watched as each of the white panelled walls around him swelled, and then slowly pushed outwards. Pale floorboards formed to occupy the extra space he'd created for himself. A terrible sound of cracking stone and mortar accompanied the whole endeavour; it sounded, for all the world, like breaking bones.

He sat on his bed, trembling and exhausted.

And then the walls began to push back. Jack could feel the other rooms around him—the other souls—reacting to his efforts. It was a sensation of pressure from all sides, of being jostled by a crowd, while remaining strangely dislocated from that same crowd. Within a matter of moments, he found himself suffering from a fierce headache. A dull metallic pounding resounded in his ears, followed by a brief and sinister laugh.

Jack strode over to the curtains and pulled them open.

Red brick lay behind the windows.

He tried one of the wall hatches next, only to find a similar impenetrable barrier. He opened another hatch, and another, but could see nothing of the rooms beyond his own except their exterior brickwork. Finally, he grabbed a claw hammer from the many tools scattered across the floor and approached one of the open hatches. He hesitated a moment, then stove the hammer deep into the mortar.

White light exploded behind his eyes, stunning him momentarily: a flare of pain that seemed to shoot through his entire brain, before coalescing into a single pinpoint of agony in his left temple. He cried out, reeling backwards, and dropped the hammer. For an instant the room around him appeared to be flooded with the same excruciating illumination. The white walls and furniture fizzed like burning magnesium. Jack clasped an arm across his face.

When he lowered his arm again, everything seemed to have returned to normal. A dull ache now pulsed in the back of his head. The muscles under his chin felt raw, as if he'd wrenched his neck around. He swallowed painfully, then looked back up at the hatch. The red brick wall had vanished, leaving a newly-formed opening into the room beyond. Glaring at him through this, was a man.

"The hell do you think you're doing?" the man said.

Jack just stared up at him mutely.

For a while, the man worked his jaw left and right as though chewing things over. He was slightly older than Jack, with a grizzled chin and an unruly burst of brown hair. His gaze wandered around Jack's apartment; he frowned at the geometric wall panelling, then his attention lingered on the torture implements scattered across the floor. "What's all this for?" he said.

The walls around Jack began to turn from white to pink.

"You kinky or something?"

"It's none of your business."

The man dragged his gaze away from the iron maiden, and looked at Jack with what appeared to be growing amusement. "I'm not making any judgements, fellow. If that's your thing, then..."

"It's not what you think."

"Hey, who cares? It's Hell, right?"

"It's not kinky," Jack said.

"Yeah, fine, whatever you say." The man was looking around again. "So why did you hang yourself?"

The question startled Jack. "How did you know that?"

The man inclined his head. "Your curtain pulls," he said, "have little nooses on the ends."

Jack hadn't noticed this particular detail before. A marked increase in the temperature of his surroundings accompanied his steadily rising levels of embarrassment.

The man grinned. "Relax, will you? I knew what to look for. It all supports my theory."

"What theory?"

"That suicides always end up together down here. All the people around you killed themselves in one way or another. Knives, nooses, poison, drowning, jumpers. This whole damned crawling monstrosity of a building is packed with them."

"You..?"

"I jumped," he admitted. "Changed my mind halfway down, not that it made any difference. I'm stuck here in the house of fun with the rest of you arseholes." He scratched his head behind his ear, then looked at Jack carefully for a long moment. "So how do you feel now?"

"What do you mean?"

"Do you still want to die?"

"I'm already dead."

The man grunted. "That's just your body. I mean, do you want to continue to *exist*? You can survive down here indefinitely as long as you have the will to keep on going, and the bloody Mesmerists don't find you." He shrugged. "Or you can take other steps, pursue other...*options*."

"I want to get out of here."

The man pursed his lips. "You mean that?"

Jack nodded.

"Seriously mean it?"

"I said so, didn't I?"

"Well thank the gods for small mercies." The man closed his eyes for a moment, and then opened them. "If either of us are ever going to get out of here, I need your help. I need you to back me up, man, talk to them before it's too late."

"Talk to whom?"

"The others," he said. "Your neighbours. The god-damned suicide club who are hell bent on taking us all to our deaths. The real, non-existence, everlasting sort of death where you don't wake up again. Death of the soul sort of death. Haven't you even looked outside yet?"

"I don't know...which way—"

"That way." He jabbed a finger at the curtains. "Just move this room of yours twenty or thirty feet and you'll reach the edge of the building. Wait till Dunnings is asleep, and then just shove his bloody apartment the hell out of your way. He'll wake up, but don't let him stop you. Hell is a contest of wills. If you really want to survive down here then you're going to have to learn to trample over other people's egos." He grinned. "Fortunately for you, Dunnings is a first class arsehole. He is the epitome of arseholeness. If you could bottle arseholeness and boil it right down until all that was left was a thick crust of pure unadulterated crap at the bottom, then that would be him. "

Jack looked at the curtained wall. Now he had a name to give the presence he felt lurking behind there. *Dunnings.* He turned back to the man in the hatch. "What do I call you?"

"Gillespie," the other man said. "Robert Gillespie, but call me Bob. Do you want me to give you the knock when the arsehole drifts off?" He inclined his head towards the wall again. "Most newcomers can't sense things like that."

"Thanks." Jack hesitated. "Do you mind me asking…?"

"What? Why I did it?"

Jack nodded.

The other man sighed. "Because I was an idiot. I owed a lot of money, and…" He shook his head. "You know how it goes."

An idea occurred to Jack. "You're not from Cog, are you?" he said.

"Of course I am," Gillespie said. "Everyone here is from Cog or thereabouts. I lived in Port Sellen. The others came from Knuckletown, the Island, Highcliffe, couple of fellows from The Heights, Minnow Road, Alderney. It's like the suicide thing, there's a geographical connection to it all, too. Souls from a particular area always cluster. Which part of the city are you from?"

"Highcliffe." Jack reached his hand towards the hatch. "I'm Jack Aviso."

Gillespie recoiled. "Wait! Stop!"

Jack froze.

"This room is my *soul*, you idiot. Keep your bloody hands to yourself."

Gillespie reappeared at the hatch several hours later that day—or night. Jack had yet to determine if such concepts even existed in hell. He had been lying on his bed, trying to recall the transition between the moment of his death and his arrival here. He remembered the Complaint Wheel cabin, and the rope, and he remembered waking up, but nothing between. Gillespie had referred to him as a newcomer, but how had Jack, along with his surroundings, actually managed to become entangled among this particular group of people?

"You need to watch out for that," Gillespie said through the wall hatch.

"For what?"

"Things start moving about when you try to figure this place out. Furniture, walls, doors…before you know it, you've redecorated." He pressed a finger against the side of his head. "You've got to focus, keep everything in an ordered place, if you want to stay sane down here."

Jack realised the other man was right. Almost all of the furniture in his room had changed position. The iron maiden had moved much closer to the bed, as if it had meant to sneak up and ambush him. Many of the white panels had shifted from the walls and were now traversing the floor and ceiling, giving the whole place a kind of *upended* feel. It was quite disconcerting. "How did I come to be here?" he said. "Among all of you?"

"You killed yourself."

"No, I mean, how did I actually *arrive* here. I don't remember."

Gillespie shook his head. "We'll talk about that later. Small steps, Jack. Sort yourself out first, find your place in the hierarchy, build up your confidence. Too much knowledge at once can unhinge a man, and I need you to stay sharp." He looked over at the wall, in the direction of Dunnings's apartment. "So, are you ready to do this?"

Jack said he was.

Gillespie told him to prepare for the push in exactly the same way as one might prepare for a short but intense physical exertion. He made him face the wall he intended to move, the only section of Jack's subconscious obscured by drapes. *Deep breaths, psyche yourself up, feel your surroundings, the gentle pressures on all sides, the pulse of your sleeping neighbour's soul. Now imagine what you need to do. Your subconscious created those windows in that wall for a reason. It knew where the outside lay. Get ready...*

And push.

Jack pushed.

With a thunderous crack and roar, the wall receded by five, ten, fifteen feet. The ceiling, floor, and adjacent walls all stretched to accommodate the newly created space. He sensed the structure out with his soul crumble and break apart as he shoved his way through the bricks and mortar of his neighbour's sleeping mind.

And then suddenly he felt resistance. In the back of his own mind, he thought he heard a growl, followed by a furious roar. The window drapes started to shake violently. The receding wall slowed, stopped, and all at once the effort of his expansion became unbearable. Evidently, Dunnings had woken up, and was now fighting back.

"Don't stop now," Gillespie cried. "Shove harder!"

Jack put all of his mind's muscle into the task. He imagined he heard manic screaming coming from beyond the drapes. He bulled forwards, throwing every ounce of his will into moving the wall onwards. It crept forward another foot, then five, and then, quite suddenly, the resistance vanished. The wall shot away from him another ten feet. Behind it he could sense nothing but air.

He slumped on the bed, exhausted, his nerves raw and twitching with a thousand new sensations.

Gillespie clapped his hands. "Well done, son," he said. "You see how easy it is when you put your mind to it?"

"That…wasn't…easy."

"Course it was easy," Gillespie said. "I told you Dunnings was an arsehole. Now draw back the curtains, and take a look at where you are. Just try not to panic, will you?"

The curtains, along with the wall itself, now stood some forty feet away from Jack. His efforts had significantly increased the size of the apartment. And yet even now he could sense Dunnings's disapproval. The brickwork lurking behind the right-hand side of the room seemed to throb with anger.

"What are you waiting for? Go on, I'll meet you out there."

Out there?

Jack got to his feet, shakily. He crossed his apartment and stood before the curtains. Then he drew them back.

Beyond the windows boiled a sky as hot and red as furnace metal, its horizons bruised by reefs of smouldering crimson cloud. He was looking down from a height of three or four storeys across a sinuous maze of blood red canals and interconnected pools, gruesome fluidways that formed loops and whorls between endless tiers of black stone walls, arches, and towers. Rotten temples and huge dark ziggurats rose from flooded quadrangles amidst the ragged stumps of pillars and smashed colonnades, while here and there great piles of broken stonework loomed over the surrounding morass, glistening like mountains of wet anthracite. Even the air itself looked damp and unwholesome, curried by mists and columns of red vapour.

Jack took a step back, instinctively covering his nose, before he spotted Gillespie. His neighbour was standing outside, on a balcony to the right of Jack's own apartment, gesturing at him to open the window.

Jack shook his head.

Gillespie mouthed something incomprehensible. He gestured again, this time with greater insistence.

Jack laid a hand on the window handle. He took a deep breath and then opened it.

A breeze wafted in, warm and wet and carrying a rich iron odour. It reminded him of the alleyways behind the butchers' shops in Knuckletown. A low rumbling sound came from somewhere below the window.

"...to create a balcony," Gillespie said.

Jack peered down. A confusion of different architectural styles made up the façade below,

various faces of brick, stone and ironwork all crushed together into an unregulated mess. Most of it looked stained—or perhaps burnt—black. A nest of canals separated by dense stone walls stretched out around the base of the building, the bloody waters shining dully in the uncertain light. He could not locate the source of the noise. "What did you say?" he said to Gillespie.

"I said, you just need to think of stepping out onto a balcony, and your mind will create one."

"I don't want one," Jack said.

The other man spread out his hands in a gesture of resignation. "Suit yourself," he said. "But if you want to get out of this place, you'd better get used to altering your own environment. You think you can just climb down this wall without protection? The shock of leaving all this—" he slapped a hand on the balustrade "—would snap your mind."

Jack recalled the warning in Marley's book. If his immediate physical surroundings were actually defensive barriers created by the core of his soul, then he could not simply step outside without leaving himself vulnerable. To escape from his own dwelling in Hell was not possible. In order to travel, he had to bring his apartment with him.

The floor under him jolted suddenly, nearly knocked him of his feet.

"Tremors," Gillespie said. "You never notice them until you can see the ground below. Some trick of the subconscious, I suppose. Filters it out. But you feel them as soon as you're reminded that the building is moving."

Jack glanced down, and realised that the whole structure had moved several feet since he'd last checked. Indeed, it was still moving now, sliding ever so slowly over the surface of Hell. He heard a further rumbling sound coming from the foundations, followed by the subterranean trickle of fluids, and the whole building obscured another inch of that blood-slicked, treacherous ground.

Gillespie pointed down at the landscape. "So, you see what's ahead of us?"

At first Jack could see nothing but the labyrinth of fluid-ways and twisting walls, the clutching silhouettes of countless ruined structures rising from pools as red as wounds. And then he spotted something moving down there: a long, dark shape in one of the canals. As he watched, he began to notice others in the gauzy distance—boats, or barges, and they were manned. Hunched white figures moved about on their decks.

"Mesmerists," Gillespie said. "Those ones are Icarates, Menoa's own soul collectors. You see that tower where the canals converge? It's one of their collection depots. They bring souls there before shipping them back to their boss."

Jack spotted the tower about half a league away. A vicious collection of stone spikes, it looked far less ruinous and far more purposeful than the neighbouring structures. It stood on arched foundations over the junction of at least seven canals, like a great black thorn tree. "What happens to the souls brought there?" he asked.

"You don't want to know," Gillespie replied. "But I'll tell you anyway. Menoa boils them up and changes them into whatever he needs, whether it's a brick or a roof tile for one of his citadels, or a sword for one of his uglier *creations*. And that's the very place our neighbours want to take us. The idiots think that if they give themselves over to the Lord of the Maze, they won't have to suffer any more of this." He jabbed his thumb at the apartment behind him. "A sword doesn't have to think, does it?"

Fear gripped Jack. The tower was *too* close, and he wasn't nearly ready to undertake his escape. His plan might take weeks to prepare, but by the look of things he had mere days left. "We have to stop this building," he said.

Gillespie grunted. "Yes we do," he said. "But that's easier said than done. You'll see what I mean when you speak to the others."

Gillespie's idea was to call a residents' meeting. Perhaps he and Jack together could talk some sense into the others? Failing that, the pair of them might attempt to disrupt the forward progress of the building by a combined effort.

After his somewhat removed yet violent encounter with Dunnings, Jack didn't particularly want to meet the rest of his neighbours. Gillespie referred to them as *The Suicide Club,* or *The Biggest Bunch of Cheerless Halfwits it's Ever Been My Misfortune to Meet,* or sometimes just *Those Arseholes.* He explained that there was a neutral territory in the heart of the building, a chamber where all the neighbours could speak to one another. He called this place *The Room of Gloom,* and said that Jack would have to make some further alterations to his surroundings in order to access it.

"You need to create a tunnel," he explained through the hatch. "The narrower, the better, since there's no space whatsoever inside this building. You'll have to jostle with the other consciousnesses in here, shove them about a bit. I'll guide you, so you cause minimal damage. I've already warned everyone to let you through, but we don't want to aggravate anyone more than we need to."

"What about Dunnings?" Jack said. "He's already furious."

"Sod him," Gillespie said.

Under Gillespie's guidance, Jack began the process of creating a passageway from his own quarters to *The Room of Gloom*. First, he created a small door in the inner wall of his apartment. Then he lay down on his bed with his eyes closed, and attempted to reach out beyond that door. It was like trying to stretch out his hand without actually moving his hand. After a few false starts, he finally got the hang of it, and soon sensed a tunnel forming like a tendril outside his apartment. It helped to visualise the conduit as a root or a branch growing out of his own consciousness, which is essentially what it was. He could feel the other dwellings shifting around him as he extended this new ghost limb. He probed and prodded, directing his will into the smallest gaps between neighbouring souls, and then gently forcing them apart. Walls and ceilings trembled, but they shifted grudgingly, just as Gillespie said they would.

Finally, Gillespie told him to stop. The passageway had reached its destination.

"Now imagine a window at the far end," he said.

"What sort of window?"

The other man rolled his gaze skywards. "Whatever the hell sort of window you like. Make it out of studded leather for all I care. I've already summoned the others. I'll meet you down there." His unruly mop of hair vanished from the hatch.

Jack opened the door he'd made.

The corridor wasn't exactly as he'd intended. A rectangular metal conduit spiralled down into darkness, more like a hotel laundry chute than a passageway designed for people. The sides felt smooth and cool to the touch. Feeling slightly embarrassed, he gripped the door lintel, slid his legs into the chute and balanced himself on the edge. Then he eased himself forward and let go.

He careered downwards at at alarming rate, his shoulders thumping against the sides of the chute at every twist and turn. At one point, the floor dropped away at such a steep angle he found himself airborne briefly before he slammed back down again. And then all of a sudden the soles of his shoes smacked against something solid, and he stopped.

He was in a tiny spherical chamber, featureless but for a single grille set low in the wall. It reminded him of the ones in his former workplace. Jack got to his feet, but found that he couldn't stand upright in this confined space. He crouched before the grille and peered through.

The opening looked out into a cylindrical room with a round table in its centre. On the table sat a single plate of rather unpleasant-looking biscuits. The room was otherwise empty, without any chairs or other furniture. An assortment of different portals—at least a score of open windows and hatches of various sizes—overlooked the table from even intervals around the curved walls. Behind most of these was a face.

He spotted Gillespie to his immediate right, but he didn't recognise the others. They varied in age and appearance. Among them: a nervous, pink-cheeked lad seated behind the window to his left; a rotund woman with sticks in her hair, and wearing a tangerine dress so bright and vile it offended nature itself; a dark-haired wisp of a girl with a washed-out complexion and mournful, hollow eyes; a tweedy gentleman framed in Florian style buck woodwork; a couple of miners with seamed and gravelly faces; and a tiny blackbird of a spinster who peered out of a square portal next to Gillespie with murderous suspicion. Apart from himself and Gillespie, Jack counted nineteen others in total: nine men and ten women. Only one of the windows was empty.

"Dunnings couldn't make it," Gillespie said to Jack, with a grin. "He's probably still pissed."

"No doubt he had good reason," the spinster said. "Don't think I don't know what you're up to, Robert Gillespie. Your ridiculous schemes won't work on us."

"No schemes, Ariel," Gillespie said. "I just wanted to introduce you all to our newest resident. This is Jack Aviso."

The old woman regarded Jack with knife-blade eyes.

"What's the point?" the boy said wearily. "Nobody cares any more." He sniffed and rubbed a hand under his nose, and then gazed despondently at the table.

"Welcome to the carnival of fun," Gillespie said to Jack. "That's Charley, this is Morwena, Glynn, Sally, Bob Two, Harold, Mr and Mrs Clifford, Regina, Ariel, Doctor Shula, Ron, Lisa, Hope, Sandy and Mo, Beaker—don't ask me why, John, and Clementine there with the dark hair." He indicated each with his finger. "Doctor Shula, the Cliffords, and Ariel all lived in Highcliffe, too. Morwena and Charley are from Port Sellen. The others…here and there…The Heights, Sillbank, all over the place." He flourished a hand. "Bob Two was in the navy, drowned himself. The doc used pills. Clementine cut her wrists, of course. And Ariel—"

"That's personal," the spinster said. "I don't want you bandying it about."

"I'm sorry, Ariel," Gillespie said. "I thought you might like to know that you and Jack have something in common." He turned to Jack, sticking out his tongue while tugging at an imaginary rope above his neck.

"Hello," Jack said.

"Can we go now?" the young, dark-haired girl said. "I really don't feel up to this today."

"Five minutes, Clementine," Gillespie said. "Please."

She shook her head, tears suddenly brimming in her eyes. "These meetings are hard for me."

"Well—"

"No, you don't know," she cried. She took a shaky breath. "I don't even…have…" And then the sobs came gushing out in great breathless surges from the pit of her lungs. "I don't…ha…ha…ah…" She grabbed her head in clenched hands and began to wail miserably.

The boy, Charley, gave her a look that managed to encompass both pity and a desperate yearning. "Clementine," he said. "I understand. We all understand."

"Ah…ah…ah…"

Gillespie muttered under his breath. "For heaven's sake."

As Clementine's sobs filled the chamber, the gentleman in tweeds said, "This really is pointless. I'm going back to my quarters. None of us have any intention of prolonging our misery more than is necessary."

"Come on, Doc," Gillespie said. "You haven't even heard us out."

"So you *were* scheming?" Ariel said.

"I'm not *scheming*, Ariel," Gillespie said. "I'm trying to save your life. All of our lives."

"This isn't life!" she cried. "It's nothing but pain and struggle. It's *worse* than it was back in Pandemeria, because it's *endless*."

Doctor Shula said, "I'm sorry you've been caught up in this, Bob, I truly am. But we voted, twice, and you have to respect the group's final decision."

"Are you *all* from Cog?" Jack asked.

A few heads nodded behind windows. Others just stared miserably at the floor. Doctor Shula looked over. "Bob has his own agenda," he said to Jack. "Don't let him talk you into anything you don't want to do. We have decided—almost unanimously—to take our chances with the Mesmerists, and end our existence here."

"You *all* committed suicide?"

"As did you, I presume," the doctor said.

Jack nodded. "But I'm curious to know," he said. "How many of you are here as a result of my former boss? Mr Henry Sill."

From the number of hostile looks he received from behind those other windows and hatches, Jack guessed that a considerable number of these wretches had had some sort of relationship with the Henry Sill Banking Corporation. It seemed that Gillespie's Theory of Association extended beyond mere similarities in the method, and geographical location, of one's death. Jack wondered if that was why *he* in particular had ended up as Gillespie's neighbour, since they were, apparently, the only two who did not wish to perish a second time. At Jack's comment, Gillespie hung his head in despair, as though his only flicker of hope had just been extinguished.

Doctor Shula's grey eyes hardened. "Mr Sill is responsible for a great deal of suffering," he said. "I doubt this is the only one of hell's Middens born from his victims."

"But aren't you furious?" Jack said. "Don't you *want* justice?"

Charley said, "Who's going to give you justice down here? Menoa doesn't care about the world of the living. All we can hope for is oblivion."

"But Henry Sill is dead," Jack said. "He's here, in hell."

Silence filled the room. Even Clementine stopped sobbing. Everyone stared at Jack.

"That's why I put a rope around my neck," Jack explained. "I came here to find him and to make him suffer for what he did to me." He heard his own voice start to waver. "He took my wife from me for no reason except to satisfy his own greed, and I'm going to make him pay for that."

"Are you sure about this?" one of the miners said.

"I saw his body myself."

A new look of hope came into Gillespie's eye. "He died in Cog?"

Jack nodded.

"When?"

"Sixteen months ago."

"Then he can't be far away," Gillespie said to the others.

"Wait a minute," Doctor Shula said. "We have already decided on a course of action here. Let's not be swayed by what-ifs and…conjecture. If Mr Sill *is* actually dead, there's no reason to assume we could ever find him in this labyrinth. For all you know the Mesmerists might already have him."

"He came here to confer with the Mesmerists," Jack said. "He had some sort of proposal to put to King Menoa. But he's still running his business from somewhere down here. The bank has a machine they use to communicate with his soul in Hell."

The miners exchanged a glance. Most of the others looked thoughtful. The sad-eyed woman pursed her lips, while Clementine's rubbed the tears from her eyes. Charley had lost his air of despondency. And even Ariel seemed to be considering the possibilities.

"He's running his corporation *from Hell?*" one of the miners said through clenched teeth.

Jack nodded.

Gillespie said, "I think we should take another vote."

Doctor Shula raised his hands. "It's too late for that, Bob."

"But we have a chance to get the bastard," the miner said.

His comrade nodded in agreement.

"He took my house," the miner went on. "He forced me to push his fucking carts and breathe rock dust until I dropped."

"His Reclamation Men took everything from me," Ariel said. "The furniture, the carpets, even the taps. Forty years of savings, gone."

"He stole my boys' inheritance," said another man.

"My mother took a loan from him," Charley said. "He… I couldn't help her. They wouldn't even listen to me."

The sad-eyed woman leaned forward. "He sold my daughter."

The group fell silent. Jack could see from their faces that he had already won the majority of them over to his cause.

"Shall we vote?" Gillespie said. "Please raise your hand if you are in favour of finding Mr Henry Sill, and having a quiet word with him."

LEAVING THE CONFINES
OF A MIDDEN OR OTHER
COMMINGLED STRUCTURE

ROM HIS WINDOW JACK could see that the building had altered course. The combined wills of its residents were now moving this whole ugly conglomeration of souls away from the Icarate depot. He stood for several minutes behind the glass, watching the barges plying the canals, the red mists drifting like gossamer veils across endless furrows of black stone, and it occurred to him that this entire landscape had to have been formed by the expectations of the damned. Hell appeared this way because those who dwelt here expected it to be like this. Jack's own apartment reflected his subconscious desires, using them to construct a barrier against the turmoil outside. But that turmoil was itself composed of souls, many of whom had evidently lost their own defences. Fluid held no structure of its own, but simply occupied whatever space was imposed by the constraints around it. He wondered what Mr Henry Sill's place of residence would be like.

Finding the banker was going to be a problem. Gillespie's theory of association predicted he would be somewhere reasonably close by, but it still left them with untold leagues of maze to search. To make matters worse, Mr Sill would be hidden inside some type of structure. And they had no means of searching inside such places yet. Jack decided it was time to implement the most difficult and dangerous part of his plan. He summoned Marley's book, and turned to the appropriate section.

Section Twenty Three
Leaving the Confines of a Midden or Other Commingled Structure

It is extremely dangerous for the Conscious Soul to leave the protection of its domicile. However, it is theoretically possible to extricate that same domicile from its neighbouring structures, and convey it across the surface of hell in a snail-like fashion. The difficulty lies in convincing the mind, which retains subconscious awareness of the physical limitations of its former body, to accept that such a seemingly super-human feat is possible. Some Cog University Scholars have postulated that this may be achieved in one of two ways: through the use of mesmerism; or by wilfully reducing the size of one's domicile to more manageable proportions. It must be noted that both methods invoke serious risk, particularly the latter, wherein one's defences would be woefully diminished. In such a case, the Conscious Soul risks being crushed within the Commingled Structure.

Jack lay on the floor as he prepared to attempt the latter. He closed his eyes and allowed his senses to roam through the floorboards and the walls and the glass. He envisaged his surroundings as a cocoon connected to his body by a web of the threads, which he then he began to draw inwards. A great rumbling and crackling sound came from all around as wood snapped and glass shattered. The pain forced a cry from his lips, but he did not stop.

"What the hell are you doing?"

Jack recognised Gillespie's voice. He opened his eyes to see his neighbour peering in through his usual hatch.

"You're not giving up?" Gillespie cried. "Not now?"

Jack ignored him. He could sense the other apartments all around him, swelling to fill the extra space he was creating around his own shrinking rooms. Even Gillespie's chamber seemed to push against his own, perhaps driven by the other man's natural instinct. As the walls closed in on Jack they began to change in colour and texture, from a geometric array of painted white panels to the smooth hard expanse of metal.

"You'll be crushed," Gillespie said.

Jack gasped. "It's the only way to get Sill."

"Sill?" Gillespie frowned. "No, you…we'll use absorption, Jack. We'll…"

But then the hatch vanished, swallowed by the contracting, buckling walls.

Jack concentrated on the windows, drawing them ever closer to his aching body. Splinters of glass loomed over his head, the broken squares no longer full of fuming red skies, but dark with views of brickwork and iron. He reformed the glass into solid pane, then howled with the agony of them snapping again. Shattering and reforming, shattering and reforming. He fought to keep structure in this crumbling miasma of wood and dust. The furniture? He imagined the bed and dresser melting like so much ice, and then flowing into the floor, hardening, turning into the polished steel of his design. The torture implements followed, the iron maiden dissolving into a pool of metal.

The coal scuttle, the chair, his wife's portrait, he absorbed them all into this new liquid form. The chromic corners of his rapidly diminishing apartment began to curve. He shaped them with his will, forming plates that slid against each other, then snapped abruptly into the correct position. He screwed his eyes shut and reached out his arms and touched cold steel: the steel of a sphere, the steel of a coffin.

And finally, the steel of an armoured suit.

He was fully encased from fist to toe in tightly fitting metal plates. The windows he'd once peered out of, and then fractured and remade so many times, now formed a thick glass faceplate about four inches high. Jack pushed his nose against it. He tried to turn his head, but it wouldn't budge. He tried to lift his arms, to no avail. In a moment of blind panic, he struggled like a caged animal, thrashing his limbs against the inside of the suit. But it was hopeless. He was trapped, completely pinned between the walls of his neighbour's apartments.

Gillespie's voice came from somewhere above. "You bloody idiot."

A bead of sweat made its way across Jack's brow, and then trickled down his cheek and neck. Beyond the faceplate he could see nothing but a sliver of red brick illuminated by some overhead source of light. He struggled to raise his head up towards the voice, but the helmet remained firmly locked where it was.

"Now you're really stuffed," Gillespie said. "How do you expect to get out of there?"

"It seemed like a good idea at the time," Jack said.

"Why didn't you listen to what I was saying?" Gillespie remarked. "I told you we'll get the bloody banker through *absorption*."

Absorption? Gillespie had mentioned something about that, now that Jack thought about it.

"How do you think *you* ended up here?" Gillespie said. "You didn't just wake up here, fully formed, by accident. This building *absorbed* your soul. *The collective* absorbed your soul. It's how like minds end up together. Your spirit latched on to us, we accepted you at some subconscious level, and so you started to grow among us. And *that's* how we'll get Sill. Once we find him, the collective will accept him. Because we outnumber him, we'll absorb his whole damn building, trap it in here with us."

"And then what?"

"Then we get out the sledgehammers."

Jack struggled to move, but soon gave up again. "How do you plan to find him in the first place?"

Gillespie grunted. "What was it you told me? *You are your own surroundings.* Sill's soul won't be tangled up in a Midden full of commoners. Who would have him? So we look for an *individual structure*, a solitary design. It's likely to be something grand, the sort of place a banker would imagine for himself. You didn't have to go and get yourself crushed."

"Sorry."

He heard Gillespie sigh. "Do you feel strong enough to push the walls back? Can you get yourself out?"

"I don't think so."

Gillespie sighed again. "I'll have to speak to Dunnings. This is going to take a combined effort."

Jack waited for what felt like hours, listening to the sound of his own cavernous breathing inside his helmet. The glass faceplate steamed up, until he could see nothing at all through it. His nose itched, but he couldn't reach up to scratch it, so he rubbed it against the inside of his helmet. And all the while he could feel the texture of the surrounding bricks through this living metal prison he'd created. He sensation was akin to sensing pressure through one's teeth.

Eventually, he heard Gillespie's voice again. "You'll be pleased to know that Dunnings is pissing himself," he said. "He thinks it's hilarious."

"Will he help get me out?"

"He'll do it, but there's a condition. He doesn't want you next door to him any more. You've made this suit of armour, so you're stuck with it now. He wants you out of the building."

"That *was* my plan."

Gillespie was silent for a long moment, then spoke in a kinder voice: "That suit's not going to offer you much protection out there," he said. "The metal is full of nerves, or whatever passes for nerves down here. You'd have been better off sticking with us."

"It's becoming hard to breathe."

"Just a minute."

Jack flexed his muscles, readying them to move. Moments later he felt the pressure outside his suit begin to relax. Suddenly he could move his arm. His foot shifted. And then light poured in. He saw the wall behind his faceplate retract. It leaned away from him. He slid down several feet, then stopped. Gillespie had been right about the armour. It was merely an extension of his own skin. Jack could feel the wall grating against him *through* his metal boots. But he found that he was able to turn his shoulders. Through the foggy glass he saw that he was in a brick defile, or a narrow cave. Ten feet away, a thin, leaf-shaped opening looked out upon the steaming labyrinth of hell. Carefully, he made his way towards it.

Gillespie was standing on his balcony, to the left of the cave entrance. "You've just undergone a major transformation," he said. "You should get some rest before you try growing another room for yourself."

Jack gazed out at the endless expanse of bloody canals. "I'm fine the way I am."

"Don't be mad. We're not kicking you out. You can create another place among us."

"But Dunnings said—"

The other man made a hissing noise. "Only an idiot would expect you to keep that promise," he said. "What's he going to do if you stay?" He shook his head. "Get yourself up on the roof, son, and start thinking about some proper protection."

The brickwork to Jack's left began to bubble, and a score of small protrusions popped out of its uneven surface. The protrusions reformed into the rungs of a ladder, leading up to the roof of Gillespie's dwelling.

"I'll stay with you until we find him," Jack said. "That's all."

Gillespie simply shook his head again.

And so it came to pass that Jack found himself atop what Doctor Shula had called a Midden, a conglomeration of souls crawling across the surface of Hell. He sat there in his skin metal suit and watched the ever-changing naphtha skies and the tortuous red fluidways and he listened to the crackle and grind of the building's foundations and the gurgle of liquids passing through hollow spaces. The pulsing crimson knot that was not a sun never moved from its position in the centre of the heavens, and yet over time it grew steadily darker and then lighter again. Jack accepted these fluctuations as days and nights, although it never became truly dark. Hell simply cycled between degrees of twilight.

The Midden's roof space, like its façades, was a mash of different styles, with slopes of brick and pebble stones and odd little ramps of slate that collided in wavelike crests and troughs. You could see the lines where the residents' consciousnesses met. There were chimneys that seemed to breathe and mutter when Jack stooped to listen closely. The whole jumble reacted to his presence in subtle ways, sometimes bending, sometimes bruising under his boots, sometimes shifting violently as though it meant to pitch him off altogether.

He watched it all from the confines of his suit, which he never really got used to. He soon discovered that scratching his nose with his hand was impossible, even with his limbs now free. The sound of his breathing constantly hissed and boomed in his own ears. Metal clanked whenever he walked, and yet he dimly sensed the texture of his surroundings under his metalled palm and through the soles of his boots. He found himself sweating a lot, and was forced to suffer the countless trickles of perspiration with flinching eyes.

Often he sat on the edge of the Midden and chatted with Gillespie, who came out on to his balcony to relay progress and gossip. No one had spotted an individual dwelling thought likely to contain the errant banker, but Jack nevertheless took these opportunities to learn more about his neighbours. Gillespie had owned a small business in Port Sellen making wooden frames for paintings and lithographs. He'd never married, but had narrowly escaped it twice, he claimed. He'd

had a dog called Ginger, a Reiger Spaniel, whom he talked about with great affection. Dunnings had been a tax collector, which explained much of Gillespie's (and, indeed, the whole group's) animosity towards him. Clementine had hoped to study drama at one of the city theatres and begged her parents to borrow the necessary funds, with tragic consequences. The spinster Ariel had lost her fortune, along with her house in Highcliffe, mere days after her husband, Max, had died in suspicious circumstances. She hadn't poisoned him, she swore. Charley had been all set on a naval career, joining the Port Sellen Cadets some months before his mother's unfortunate dealings with the bank changed things. Doctor Shula specialised in repairing bones and made miniature locomotives from sheets of tin. He'd lived on Hill Wynd with a young actor called Michael.

Jack wondered if Carol was down here somewhere, too. Part of him yearned to abandon his desire to see justice done, and use his new found freedom to search for her. But yet another part of him rejected this idea, for it was this aspect of Hell more than any other that made any future he might have here unbearable. Even if *could* find her, they would never truly be together again. They'd simply exist as two imprisoned souls, unable to touch, to hold hands, condemned to simply gaze at each other from behind their own defences. To do otherwise would be a painful violation of the other person.

Would oblivion be preferable? He would think on that some more.

His attempt to gain liberty through the suit of armour had not been a complete failure. After all, he could now move around outside the Midden, even if it had left him more vulnerable than he'd anticipated. The protection of a more substantial dwelling was all very well, if one accepted that existence was nothing more than a series of rooms.

It was shortly before twilight on the seventeenth day when Gillespie called up excitedly from his balcony: "Jack? Are you up there? Look to the north."

"Which way is north?"

"Towards the sun. It has to be Sill's home."

Jack wandered over to the edge of the Midden and looked out. Out there in the distance, he could see a dark grey tower rising above the tangled bloodwork. It was by far the largest structure in sight: smooth-walled, but with a pronounced list to one side as though it might topple over and come crashing to the ground at any moment. A bulb of stone adorned its summit (featureless but for a single narrow window, or murderhole), while from its base extruded two small, compact structures that Jack took to be gatehouses.

Gillespie called from below: "Do you see it?"

"How do you know it's his?" Jack shouted back.

Gillespie sputtered. "Are you *serious*?"

Jack bit down on his lip. Henry Sill might indeed have imagined such an edifice to protect his soul, for it exuded not just strength and power, but a vulgar sort of dominance over the surrounding landscape. The crown was fist-like, threatening, its murderhole dark, and yet seemingly watchful—as though it might at any moment eject some vile and poisonous fluid upon the glutinous soils of Hell.

"It's possible," Jack conceded.

He heard Gillespie mutter something in response, but he could not make out the words.

It took them two more days to reach the tower. During that time, Jack watched it grow until it filled the sky. The whole edifice sat back from all of the surrounding canals, in its own flooded quadrangle. As they drew nearer, Jack spotted a coat of arms carved into the lower wall, and his heart quickened as he recognised the stylised coin and garrotte of the Henry Sill Banking Corporation. The gatehouses, he now saw, possessed no gates or openings in them at all, but had been fortified with thousands of vicious iron spikes. And it appeared that a battle had taken place around it, for the walls, temples and arches so prevalent in other parts of Hell were not in evidence here; leaving in their place a wasteland of bloody pools and shattered rock.

The Midden came to a stop about a hundred yards from the tower, whereupon Gillespie summoned Jack over to the edge of the roof. He looked troubled.

"There's been some discussion about the whole…absorption process," he said. "The long and short of it is…" He hesitated, leaning back against his balcony balustrade. "Well, it seems that most of the residents are cooling to the whole idea. They're not entirely convinced it's going to work."

"You want me to go in alone?" Jack said.

Gillespie shook his head. "Give me some time with them. It's just cold feet, you know—"

"I'm happy to go in alone."

Gillespie looked up at him. "That place isn't like the others down here," he said. "It's simply too massive to have been created by a single man's soul. I think—the group thinks—that someone down here helped him."

"You mean King Menoa?"

Gillespie nodded. "If Sill came here to do business with the Mesmerists, then it may be that he succeeded. Menoa's

Icarates rip through whatever defences we create to capture the minds hiding inside. The king then subjugates those minds and uses them to sculpt vast, living citadels." He inclined his head towards the tower. "If he's done the same thing here for our Mr Sill, then you're not going to stand a chance in there. That tower might contain half a million souls, all enslaved to the banker's own will. If he detects an intruder, he'll use those souls to tear you apart."

Jack thought about this. If Gillespie was right, then the planned absorption wouldn't work either. The souls inside that listing tower must vastly outnumber their own, which meant that it would be the Midden residents themselves who'd end up absorbed and trapped inside Henry Sill's defences. They would be at his mercy, rather than the other way around.

He couldn't allow that to happen.

But he couldn't turn away, either.

There had to be a way to penetrate the banker's defences. Hell was just a system like any other—complex, insane, and unfair, but a system nevertheless. And Jack had worked with systems all of his life. He gazed up at the massive structure, at the smooth, unscalable walls unbroken by door or window, at the ghastly iron defences.

"Thank the others for me," he said.

"What are you doing, Jack?"

"I'm going to find Mr Henry Sill, and bring him back."

And then he walked over to the edge of the roof and started climbing down.

THE LEANING TOWER

J ACK WADED THROUGH THE flooded quadrangle under the shadow of Henry Sill's tower. He could feel the chill red fluid through his steelskin boots; it sucked at his ankles and shins with an almost sentient insistence, causing him to shudder with every step. Occasionally he sensed objects shift underfoot—broken scraps of stone, or perhaps the bone of a long dead combatant—but he did not linger to investigate.

He passed between the gatehouses, huffing inside his metal suit, and strolled right up to the main shaft of the tower itself.

This façade afforded him no obvious entrance. Its stones were so precisely cut and arrayed that even the keenest of knives would not have found passage between them. Jack ran the back of his gauntlet across the featureless grey surface. Every nerve within the living steel informed him of the wall's near perfect lubricity. But he could also sense the myriad souls within it, the tremor of a million thoughts racing through the structure. He gazed up, past the coat of arms, to the great fist of stone atop its leaning summit. He could not see the murderhole from down here, but the hairs prickling on the back of his neck insisted he was being watched. A vast silence hung over this place, so dense

and pregnant with expectation that it might have been a pause in Hell's own heartbeat.

Jack turned around, leaned back against the tower, and took a deep breath. This edifice had been built to keep the likes of him outside the banker's soul. It would not accept him, not in his current form.

He remade his armoured suit, turning it from steel to gold.

The tower reacted instantaneously. Jack's vision darkened as the wall behind him flowed outwards, enveloping his arms, torso and legs. It swallowed him entirely, sucking him deep inside. For a moment it seemed to Jack that a multitude of hands were clutching lustily at his body. He sensed their overwhelming desire to possess him, and understood that it was Sill's own greed transmitted through their enslaved minds. He resisted the urge to fight, allowing himself to be drawn deeper into the bubbling mass of the banker's defences.

And then, quite suddenly, golden light filled his faceplate. The grasping hands retreated, leaving him standing in a space so bright and vast that his head rolled with vertigo. He closed his eyes and flung out his arms, and stood there for a long dizzy moment before his lurching nerves finally steadied themselves.

The interior of the tower glittered with gold. Gold coins covered the entire floor, rising up to form bluffs and hills and then vast shimmering mountains. In places the coins had been stacked into towers, some four or five feet high, but the huge bulk of this treasure simply lay in great gleaming heaps several storeys high. Jack stooped to pick up a coin.

Emblazoned upon its yellow surface was the image of a coin. He turned it over, only to discover an identical design imprinted on the other side. It seemed to Jack that these designs were representations of the actual coin he now held in his hand, for they themselves each depicted a coin emblazoned with a coin. If you looked closely enough, the cycle repeated again: coins within coins within coins, the designs becoming ever smaller and smaller until they vanished beyond the limits of sight.

He sensed something in the coin...

A thought?

Jack shivered, and let it drop from his hand.

Yellow valleys bisected the piles of coins, meandering away in several directions. Jack chose one at random and set off, his golden boots crunching through the golden ground. Coins clicked and shifted underfoot. Beyond this sparkling landscape, grey stone walls rose upwards at the same steep angle as the tower's exterior, eventually blurring into giddy heights. He looked up to see a single column of light depending from the murderhole far overhead. The sheer scale of it all afflicted him with awe.

He walked around one shining mound, and passed between two others, heading for what he judged to be the centre of the tower. He found that it was difficult to keep his balance as he walked. His boots crunched into the yielding ground or else slid across it. He displaced coins constantly, often staggering down shallow slopes with rivulets of metal trickling down behind him.

After a while he heard a faint moaning sound.

Jack followed the noise until it lead him to a broad expanse of open ground between the mountains of currency.

In the centre of this space stood a simple wooden table. On a stool behind this table sat the founder of the Henry Sill Banking Corporation.

He wore the same dark suit his own corpse had worn. This incarnation of the man, like the desiccated one still lying on the bed in the Hotel Margareta, possessed no hands. However, during his time in Hell, in appeared that Henry Sill had suffered an additional and equally gruesome alteration to his person, for the man Jack saw before him now lacked a mouth. The part of his face beneath his nose was completely smooth, without any opening through which he might eat or speak. These adaptations to his physical form were clearly causing him much distress, as he hunched over a wooden bowl set on the table before him. He was trying to use a knife he'd somehow managed to clamp between the stumps of his wrists to shovels coins from the bowl towards the place where his mouth had once been.

Jack walked towards him.

Henry Sill glanced up in Jack's direction, perhaps alerted by the clinking currency beneath the approaching man's boots. The banker managed to emit a stifled moan, and yet his eyes remained completely blank, seemingly oblivious to Jack's presence. He lowered his head again, and went back to his knife and his bowl of coins.

Jack stood nearby and watched with a kind of morbid fascination. For every hundred attempts the banker made to lift a coin towards his sealed jaw, he must have failed ninety nine times—his efforts endlessly frustrated by both his lack of hands, and the difficulty of using such an unsuitable implement for the job. Either he dropped the knife, and had to fumble around for at eternity to retrieve it, or he successfully managed to hold the knife but failed time and again to balance a coin upon its narrow blade. And even when he finally managed to accomplish both feats together, he often dropped the coin before he could get it anywhere near his jaw. After each failed attempt, he wailed miserably and beat his stumps against the table.

It was only in those rare instances where stump, knife and coin all came together through a mixture of determination and lucky happenstance that the banker managed to raise the coin all the way up to his face. Whenever that happened, something extraordinary occurred. The knife punctured the flesh where his mouth ought to have been. By tilting his head back, balancing the coin against his nose, and working the knife deeper into his jaw, Henry Sill was able to create a wide enough opening in which to deposit the coin. He gave a grunt of pleasure through this newly made facsimile of a mouth, then promptly swallowed the coin.

At which point his opening in his face vanished once more.

Jack watched this bizarre sequence of events for a while. If the cuts Sill made with the knife caused him any pain, he didn't show it. There was certainly no blood or scars—no indication of lasting damage—and yet the flesh looked real enough.

He approached the table and crouched down until his faceplate was mere inches from Mr Sill's mouthless visage. Even now, the banker seemed blissfully unaware of Jack's presence. Indeed, he still seemed buoyed by his last successful attempt to swallow the coin, for he hummed a merry tune.

"Mr Henry Sill?" Jack said.

Sill looked up. He stared straight through Jack for a moment, then returned to his meal.

Jack knocked the bowl from the table, scattering coins everywhere.

Henry Sill gave a grunt of surprise. Without even a glance in Jack's direction, he leapt from his stool and loped across the ground to retrieve the bowl. Once he had it gripped in the crook of his arm, he used his other stump to scoop in more coins from the endless mounds all around. After the bowl was near enough full again, he bounded back to the table, flopped down once more, and resumed his earlier efforts with the knife.

Jack knocked the bowl from the table, and then watched the banker retrieve it a second time.

"Mr Sill?"

This time the he didn't even look up.

"Mr Sill!"

No response. As Henry Sill was concerned, Jack might well have been invisible.

Jack changed his suit of armour from gold to steel again.

Henry Sill stopped scraping away at his bowl. He raised his head, and this time Jack saw that the banker's expression had twisted into a rictus of mindless rage. He flung himself from the stool like a wild beast, knocking the table, knife and bowl aside. He lunged at jack, his arms outstretched, his eyes aflame with murder.

Jack leaped back instinctively, but he wasn't quick enough. Henry Sill bulled into him, pitching them both backwards into the humus of coins. Jack landed amid a great clinking and clattering of metal, pinned under the weight of the other man's body. He kicked out wildly, sending coins clattering away in all directions, but he could not extract himself from beneath his opponent. Sill reached for Jack's faceplate, as though he meant to rip it open.

But those impotent stumps could grip nothing. Jack watched the banker's wrists glancing repeatedly off the tiny glass window before his own eyes. He felt the blows through the nerves embedded in his armour, but they were as weak as those of a child.

And then he noticed other more dangerous hands reaching for him. Overhead, a section of the tower's wall had started to deform, the stonework bulging down towards him even as he watched. It appeared to form itself in the semblance of an arm. He saw a mighty stone fist, the fingers opening...

He changed his suit from steel to gold.

The tower wall retreated at once. Henry Sill stood up, dazed and uncertain, and gazed around him. Both the table and stool lay on their sides. He loped over, and set each of them upright again. He retrieved the bowl, scooped more coins into it, and replaced it on the table. Then he scrambled across the gleaming ground to where the knife had fallen. He crouched beside it, and began the tortuous process of trying to pick it up again.

Jack got to his feet. The banker's soul had no real defences down here at all. Everything he'd ever desired now lay around him in great glittering mounds. There seemed to be precious little left of the man himself, but the greed which now caused him so much suffering. Perhaps that's all there ever had been.

Jack now thought he understood why King Menoa, Lord of Hell and Lord of the Maze, had built this edifice for Henry Sill.

He left the banker to his ghastly feast and wandered among the mountains of gold until at last he heard the sound he had hoped to find.

Clack-clacka-clack-clack-clacka-clack.

He froze, listening keenly. Silence, but then after a pause, the noise started up again.

Clack-clacka-clack-clack-clacka-clack. It sounded like typing, and it was coming from back of the tower. He followed the noise until he located its source. There, perched upon a small mound of coins, was a dusty old typewriter and a pair of severed hands.

Clacka-clack-clacka-clack.

Jack watched as the desiccated fingers tapped away at the typewriter keys. The hands themselves looked just as dead and bloodless as the corpse of the banker to which they'd once been attached. The skin was wrinkled, parchment yellow, and as dry as dust. Stubs of bones extruded from the wrists. No paper or ink had been loaded into the machine itself, leaving the type-bars clacking impotently against the bare metal platen with every strike, but then the Lord of the Maze would hardly require such physical accoutrements to send his messages back to Cog.

Jack picked up one of the hands, but then dropped it at once. His golden armour crawled with revulsion. His stomach bucked and he stifled the instinct to vomit. The boundless evil he'd sensed within those remains could not have come from the simple mind of Henry Sill. Those bloodless fingers were guided by a distant, and yet vastly more powerful force. The instant Jack had touched that hand, he knew he'd touched the black and corpulent heart that resided at the centre of Hell itself. He closed his eyes and waited until his racing heartbeat began to slow. When he opened them again he saw the hand laying on its back among the coins, striking the air with its fingers, while its twin continued to work at the keyboard. If Menoa's will was indeed behind these dead appendages, then it did not yet appear to know that Jack had displaced one of them.

But how could he retrieve the things, if he couldn't bear to touch them?

A terrible wailing noise filled the air. Jack tried to ignore it as he pressed himself flat against the section of wall through which he'd entered the tower. He took a deep breath, and then he turned his armour from gold back to steel. The wall quivered once, and then softened. It flowed outwards over him, enveloping his arms and legs and chest, and finally covering his gauntlets in which he clutched the wooden bowl containing both the knife, and the severed hands, of Henry Sill.

Gillespie's concern was reflected in the expressions of the other residents, who each sat behind their respective windows and stared at the severed hands upon the table. Even now, Henry Sill's dissociated extremities continued to twitch. One of them had, by a series of arbitrary jerks, somehow managed to escape the confines of the wooden bowl, and ended up on its back among the residents' plate of biscuits, where it fidgeted like a dying spider.

Jack thought about trying to retrieve it, but decided against it for the moment. He stood patiently beside the table in his steel suit, waiting for those around him to come to a consensus. Even Dunnings had turned up, and his dark brown eyes now peered out from under the shelf of his eyebrows with a degree of interest every bit as intense as that of his fellow residents.

Ariel leaned closer to her own window, her face evincing a mixture of fascination and disgust."I don't understand," she said. "How did his *real* hands come to be here in Hell?"

"They were sent here from Cog," Jack said. "The Lord of Hell must have made a deal with the Henry Sill Banking Corporation. Menoa managed to use Sill's own flesh as a link to the living world. It gave him total control over the corporation. In return, I imagine he promised the banker all the wealth he could ever desire."

"Why would the Lord of Hell want to run a bank?" Ariel asked.

Gillespie grunted. "Think about it, Ariel."

She continued to frown at the twitching hands.

"He wanted to extend his influence," Gillespie said. "So he needed an outpost, a place from where he would be able to inflict the greatest possible degree of suffering on mankind. Look around you, and then ask yourself how we all ended up here."

She huffed. "So Henry Sill's soul is *still* safe inside that tower?"

"It wasn't much of a soul in the first place," Jack said. "I think Menoa tricked him by building that tower. Henry Sill is trapped in there, a victim of his own greed. He's enduring far more suffering than we could ever cause him."

"But if Menoa controls the hands…" Ariel began.

"Then we need to get rid of them quickly," Gillespie replied.

Clementine had a deliciously savage look in her eyes. "Do you think they still feel pain?"

"The hands?" Jack said. "No. They're just dead flesh."

She slumped back down in her chair.

"But we've broken Hell's line of communication with the bank," he added.

Dunnings gave a bark of disapproval. "Won't make any difference," he said. "You can't hurt a corporation that big. When Sill's subordinates realise nobody's giving any orders, they'll just find another soulless bastard to replace him."

Clementine perked up again. "We could always break the fingers."

Most of the others frowned at this suggestion, with the notable exception of Charley, who simply gazed at the girl with the sort of unbridled empathy that implied he'd do the grisly task himself if he only had a hammer.

Gillespie sighed. "I think we should just throw them away and hope Menoa never finds them."

Ariel and Dunnings nodded. Gillespie glanced at the miners and then at Doctor Shula, who each added their own approval. And one by one, the residents all agreed. Clementine chewed her lip for a while, but finally bowed under pressure, and Charley was quick to follow her lead.

Gillespie turned to Jack. "Will you do the honours?"

And so the residents parted their Midden again to permit their newest neighbour to leave. Jack carried the last remains of Henry Sill to the top of the building and then flung them out across the wastes of Hell. They splashed into a small square pool, where they disappeared from sight. He remained up there for a while, gazing out through his faceplate at the endless fluidways and whorls of rotten stone while the Midden crept away from the tower. He wondered what he was going to do for the rest of eternity.

And then it hit him. The severed hands and the typewriter together formed a link to the living world. But what if the hands could no longer respond to Menoa's will?

We could always break the fingers

"Gillespie," he cried, leaping to his feet. "Stop this thing! I've got to get those hands back."

His neighbour appeared on the balcony, and frowned up at him. "What?"

"The hands," Jack said. "I need them. And we have to go back for the typewriter."

"Whatever for?"

"To write our own messages."

"But what about Menoa?"

Jack didn't care. It was a risk he was prepared to take. If this new plan worked, eternity might even turn out to be fun.